Typical

Also by Padgett Powell

Edisto (1984)

A Woman Named Drown (1987)

PADGETT

TYPICAL

POWELL

An Owl Book
Henry Holt and Company · *New York*

These stories were first published, in somewhat different form, in
The New Yorker, Grand Street, The Paris Review, Soho Square,
The Gettysburg Review, Harper's, and Esquire.

Library of Congress Cataloging-in-Publication Data
Powell, Padgett.
    Typical / Padgett Powell.—1st Owl book ed.
        p.   cm.
    "An Owl book."
    I. Title.
[PS3566.08328T9   1992]
813'.54—dc20   92-7136
                                                                    CIP

ISBN 0-8050-2111-6 (An Owl Book: pbk.)

First published in hardcover by Farrar, Straus and Giroux in 1991.

First Owl Book Edition—1992

Designed by Cynthia Krupat
Printed in the United States of America
Recognizing the importance of preserving
the written word, Henry Holt and Company, Inc.,
by policy, prints all of its first editions
on acid-free paper. ∞

10   9   8   7   6   5   4   3   2   1

For Pat Strachan

●

Typical, 3

Letter from a Dogfighter's Aunt, Deceased, 19

Mr. Irony, 31

Mr. Irony Renounces Irony, 65

The Modern Italian, 71

●

Dr. Ordinary, 103

General Rancidity, 107

Mr. Nefarious, 111

Mr. Desultory, 117

Nonprofit, 123

Miss Resignation, 127

Contents

●

Flood, 133

Kansas, 137

Texas, 141

Proposition, 143

South Carolina, 145

Florida, 147

Wait, 149

●

Wayne's Fate, 155

Fear and Infinitude, 163

Labove and Son, 169

Mr. & Mrs. Elliot and Cleveland, 177

The Winnowing of Mrs. Schuping, 191

*Truth is greatly overrated,
volition where it exists must
be protected, wanting itself
can be obliterated, some people
have forgotten how to want.*
—Donald Barthelme

Typical

I **Y**esterday a few things happened. Every day a few do. My dog beat up another dog. He does this when he can. It's his living, more or less, though I've never let him make money doing it. He could. Beating up other dogs is his thing. He means no harm by it, expects other dogs to beat him up—no anxiety about it. If anything makes him nervous, it's that he won't get a chance to beat up or be beaten up. He's healthy. I don't think I am.

For one thing, after some dog-beating-up, I think I feel better than even the dog. It's an occasion calls for drinking. I have gotten a pain in the liver zone, which it is supposed to be impossible to feel. My doctor won't say I can't feel anything, outright, but he does say *he* can't feel anything. He figures I'll feel myself into quitting if he doesn't say I'm nuts. Not that I see any reason he'd particularly cry if I drank myself into the laundry bag.

I drank so much once, came home, announced to

my wife it was high time I went out, got me a black woman. A friend of mine, well before this, got in the laundry bag and suddenly screamed at his wife to keep away from him because she had *turned* black, but I don't think there's a connection. I just told mine I was heading for some black women pronto, and I knew where the best ones were, they were clearly in Beaumont. The next day she was not speaking, little rough on pots and pans, so I had to begin the drunk-detective game and open the box of bad breath no drunk ever wants to open. That let out the black women of Beaumont, who were not so attractive in the shaky light of day with your wife standing there pink-eyed holding her lips still with little inside bites. I sympathized fully with her, fully.

I'm not nice, not too smart, don't see too much point in pretending to be either. Why I am telling anyone this trash is a good question, and it's stuff it obviously doesn't need me to tell myself. Hell, I know it, it's mine. It would be like the retired justice of the peace that married me and my wife.

We took a witness which it turned out we didn't need him, all a retired JP needs to marry is a twenty-dollar tip, and he'd gotten two thousand of those tips in his twenty years retired, cash. Anyway, he came to the part asks did anyone present object to our holy union please speak up now or forever shut up, looked up at the useless witness, said, "Well, hell, he's the only one here, and *y'all* brought him, so let's get on with it." Which we did.

This was in Sealy, Texas. We crossed the town square, my wife feeling very married, proper and weepy, not knowing yet I was the kind to talk of shagging black whores, and we went into a nice bar with a marble bartop and good stools and geezers at dominoes in the back, and we drank all afternoon on one ten-dollar bill from large frozen goblet-steins of some lousy Texas beer we're supposed to be so proud of and this once it wasn't actually terribly bad beer. There was our bouquet of flowers on the bar and my wife was in a dressy dress and looked younger and more innocent than she really was. The flowers were yellow, as I recall, the marble white with a blue vein, and her dress a light, flowery blue. Light was coming into the bar from high transomlike windows making glary edges and silhouettes—the pool players were on fire, but the table was a black hole. All the stuff in the air was visible, smoke and dust and tiny webs. The brass nails in the old floor looked like stars. And the beer was 50¢. What else? It was pretty.

She's not so innocent as it looked that day because she had a husband for about ten years who basically wouldn't sleep with her. That tends to reduce innocence about marriage. So she was game for a higher stepper like me, but maybe thinks about the cold frying pan she quit when I volunteer to liberate the dark women of the world.

I probably mean no harm, to her or to black women, probably am like my dog, nervous I won't get *the chance*. I might fold up at the first shot. I regret knowing I'll never have a date with Candice Bergen, this is in the same line of thought. Candice Bergen is my pick for the most good to look at and probably kiss and maybe all-you-could-do woman in the world. All fools have their whims. Should an ordinary, daily kind of regular person carry around desire like this? Why do people do this? Of course a lot of money is made on fools with pinups in the backs of their head, but why do we continue to buy? We'd be better off with movie stars what look like the girls from high school that had to have sex to get any attention at all. You put Juicy Lucy Spoonts on the silver screen and everybody'd be happy to go home to his faithful, hopeful wife. I don't know what they do in Russia, on film, but if the street women are any clue, they're on to a way of reducing foolish desire. They look like good soup-makers, and no head problems, but they look like potatoes, I'm sorry. They've done something over there that prevents a common man from wanting the women of Beaumont.

There are many mysteries in this world. I should be a better person, I know I should, but I don't see that finally being up to choice. If it were, I would not stop at being a better person. Who would? The girls what could not get dates in high school, for example, are my kind of people now, but *then* they weren't. I was like everybody else.

I thought I was the first piece of sliced bread to come wrapped in plastic then. Who didn't. To me it is really comical, how people come to realize they are really a piece of shit. More or less. Not everybody's the Candy Man or a dog poisoner. I don't mean that. But a whole lot of folk who once thought otherwise of themself come to see they're just not that hot. That is something to think on, if you ask me, but you don't, and you shouldn't, which it proves my point. I'm a fellow discovers he's nearly worth disappearing without a difference to anyone or anything, no one to be listened to, trying to say that not being worth being listened to is the discovery we make in our life that then immediately, sort of, ends the life and its feedbag of self-serious and importance.

I used to think niggers were the worst. First they were loud as Zulus at bus stations and their own bars, and then they started walking around with radio stations with jive jamming up the entire air. Then I realized you get the same who-the-hell-asked-for-it noise off half, more than half, the white fools everywhere you are. Go to the ice house: noise. Rodeo: Jesus. Had to quit football games. There's a million hot shots in this world wearing shorts and loud socks won't take no for an answer.

And un*like* high school, you can't make them go home, quit coming. You can't make them quit playing life. I'd like to put up a cut-list on the locker-room door to the world itself. Don't suit up today, the following:

And I'm saying I'd be in the cut myself. Check your pads in, sell your shoes if you haven't fucked them up. I did get cut once, and a nigger who was going to play for UT down the road wouldn't buy my shoes because he said they stank—a nigger now. He was goddamned right about the toe jam which a pint of foo-foo water had made worse, but the hair on his ass to say something like that to me. I must say he was nice about it, and I'm kind of proud to tell it was Earl Campbell wouldn't wear a stink shoe off me.

Hell, just take what I'm saying right here in that deal. *I'm* better than a nigger who breaks all the rushing records they had at UT twice and then pro records and on bad teams, when I get *cut* from a bad team that names itself after a tree. Or something, I've forgotten. We might have been the Tyler Rosebuds. That's the lunacy I'm saying. People have to *wake up*. Some do. Some don't. I have: I'm nobody. A many hasn't. Go to the ice house and hold your ears.

This is not that important. It just surprised me when I came to it, is all. You're a boob, a boob for life, I realized one day. Oh, I got Stetsons, a Silverado doolie, ten years at ARMCO, played poker with Mickey Gilley, shit, and my girlfriends I don't keep in a little black book but on candy wrappers flying around loose in the truck. One flies out, so what? More candy, more wrappers at the store. But one day, for no reason, or no reason I know it or can remember anything happening which it meant anything, I stopped at what I was doing and said, John Payne, you are a piece of crud. You are a common, long-term drut. *Look* at it.

It's not like this upset me or anything, why would it? It's part of the truth to what I'm saying. You can't disturb a nobody with evidence he's a nobody. A nobody is not disturbed by anything significant. It's like trying to disturb a bum by yelling *poor fuck* at him. What's new? he says. So when I said, John Payne, you final asshole, I just kept on riding. But the moment stuck. I began watching myself. I watched and proved I was an asshole.

This does not give you a really good feeling, unless you are drunk, which is when you do a good part of the proving.

I've been seeing things out of the corners of my eyes and feeling like I have worms since this piece-of-crud thing. It works like this. I'm in a ice house out Almeda, about to Alvin in fact, and I see this pretty cowboy type must work for Nolan Ryan's ranch or something start to come up to me to ask for a light. That's what I *would* have seen, before. But now it works like this: before he gets to me, before he even starts coming over, see, because I'm legged up in a strange bar thinking I'm a piece of shit and a out-of-work beer at three in the afternoon in a dump in Alvin it proves it, I see out the corner of my eye this guy put his hand in his pants and give a little wink to his buddies as he starts to come over. That's enough, whatever it means, he may think I'm a fag, or he may be one himself, but he thinks you're enough a piece of shit he can touch his dick and wink about you, only he don't know that he is winking about a known piece of shit, and winking about a known piece of shit is a dangerous thing to do.

Using the mirror over the bar about like Annie Oakley shooting backwards, I spot his head and turn and slap him in the temple hard enough to get the paint to fall off a fender. He goes down. His buddies start to push back their chairs and I step one step up and they stop.

"What's all the dick and grinning about, boys?"

On the floor says, "I cain't *see*."

"He cain't see," I tell the boys.

I walk out.

Outside it's some kind of dream. There's ten Hell's Angel things running around a pickup in the highway like a Chinese fire drill, whatever that is. In the middle by the truck is a by-God muscle man out of Charles Atlas swinging chains. He's whipping the bikers with their own motorcycle chains. He's got all of the leather hogs bent over and whining where he's stung them. He picks up a bike and drops it headfirst on the rakes. Standing there with a hot Bud, the only guy other than Tarzan not bent over and crying, I get the feeling we're some kind of tag team. I drive off.

That's how it works. Start out a piece of shit, slap some queerbait blind, watch a wrestling match in the middle of Almeda Road, drive home a piece of shit, spill the hot beer I forgot about all over the seat and my leg.

I didn't always feel this way, who could afford to? When I was fifteen, my uncle, who was always kind of my real dad, gave me brand-new Stetson boots and a hundred-dollar bill on a street corner in Galveston and said spend it all and spend it all on whores. It was my birthday. I remember being afraid of the black whores and the ones with big tits, black or white, otherwise I was a ace. In those days a hundred dollars went a long way with ladies in Galveston. I got home very tired, a fifteen-year-old *king* with new boots and a wet dick.

That's what you do with the world before you doubt yourself. You buy it, dress up in it, fuck it. Then, somehow, it starts fucking back. A Galveston whore you'd touch now costs the whole hundred dollars, for example, in other words. I don't know. Today I would rather just *talk* to a girl on the street than fuck one, and I damn sure don't want to talk to one. There's no point. I need some kind of pills or something. There must be ways which it will get you out of feeling like this.

For a while I thought about having a baby. But Brillo Tucker thought this up about fifteen years ago, and two years ago his boy whips his ass. When I heard about that I refigured. I don't need a boy whipping my ass, mine or anybody else's. That would just about bind the tit. And they'll do that, you know, because like I say they come out *kings* for a while. Then the crown slips and pretty soon the king can't get a opera ticket, or something, I don't know anything about kings.

This reminds me of playing poker with Mickey Gilley, stud. First he brings ten times as much money as anyone, sits down in new boots, creaking, and hums all his hit songs so nobody can think. He wins a hand, which it is rare, and makes this touchdown kind of move and comes down slowly and rakes the pot to his little pile. During the touchdown, we all look at this dry-cleaning tag stapled to the armpit of his vest. That's the Pasadena crooner.

I was at ARMCO Steel for ten years, the largest integrated steel mill west of the Mississippi, a word we use having nothing to do with niggers for once. It means we could take ore and make it all the way to steel. Good steel. However, I admit that with everybody standing around eating candy bars in their new Levi's, it cost more than Jap steel. I have never seen a Japanese eating a candy bar or dipping Skoal showing off his clothes. They wear lab coats, like they're all dentists. We weren't dentists.

We were, by 1980, out of a job, is what we were. It goes without saying it, that is life. They were some old-timers that just moped about it, and some middle-lifer types that had new jobs in seconds, and then us Young Turks that moped *mad*. We'd filler up and drive around all day bitching about the capitalist system, whatever that is, and counting ice houses. We discovered new things, like Foosball. Foosball was one of the big discoveries. Pool we knew about, shuffleboard we knew about, Star Wars pinball we knew about, but Foosball was a kick.

For a while we bitched as a club. We were on the ice-house frontier, Tent City bums with trucks. Then a truckload of us—not me, but come to think of it, Brillo Tucker was with them, which is perfect—get in it on the Southwest Freeway with a truckload of niggers and they all pull over outside the *Post* building and the niggers whip their *ass*. They're masons or something, plumbers. A photographer at the *Post* sees it all and takes pictures. The next day a thousand ARMCO steel workers out of a job read about themselves whipped by employed niggers on the freeway. This lowered our sail. We got to be less of a club, quick. I don't know what any of my buddies are doing now and I don't care. ARMCO was ARMCO. It was along about in here I told my wife I was off to Beaumont for black chicks, and there could be a connection, but I doubt it.

As far as I can really tell, I'm still scared of them in the plain light of day. At a red light on Jensen Drive one day, a big one in a fur coat says to me, "Come here, sugar, I got something for you," and opens her coat on a pair of purple hot pants and a yellow bra.

I say, "I know you do," and step on it. Why in hell I'd go home and pick on a perfectly innocent wife about it is the kind of evidence it convinces you you're not a prince in life.

Another guy I knew in the ARMCO club had a brother who *was* a dentist, and this guy tells him not to worry about losing his job, to come out with him golfing on Thursdays and *relax*. Our guy starts going—can't remember his name—and he can't hit the ball for shit. It's out of bounds or it's still on the tee. And the dentist who wants him to relax starts ribbing him, until our guy says if you don't shut the fuck up I'm going to put this ball down and aim it at *you*. The dentist laughs. So Warren— that's his name—puts the ball down and aims at the dentist, who's standing there like William Tell giggling, and swings and hits his brother, the laughing dentist who wants him to relax, square in the forehead. End of relaxing golf.

Another guy's brother, a yacht broker, whatever that is, became a flat hero when we got laid off because he found his brother the steel worker in the shower with his shotgun and took it away from him. Which it wasn't hard to do, because he'd been drinking four days and it wasn't loaded.

Come to look at it, we all sort of disappeared and all these Samaritans with jobs creamed to the top and took the headlines, except for the freeway. The whole world loves a job holder.

One day I drove out to the Highway 90 bridge over the San Jacinto and visited Tent City, which was a bunch of pure bums pretending to be unfortunate. There were honest-to-God river rats down there, never lived anywhere but on a river in a tent, claiming to be victims of the economy. They had elected themselves a mayor, who it turns out the day I got there was up for re-election. But he wasn't going to run again because God had called him to a higher cause, preaching. He announced this with shaking hands and wearing white shoes and a white belt and a maroon leisure suit. Out the back of his tent was a pyramid of beer cans all the way to the river, looked like a mud slide in Colombia. People took me around because they thought I was out there to *hire* someone.

I met the new mayor-to-be, who was a Yankee down here on some scam that busted, had left a lifelong position in dry cleaning, had a wife who swept their little camp to where it was smoother and cleaner than concrete. I told him to call Mickey Gilley. He was a nice guy, they both were, makes you think a little more softly about the joint. How a white woman from Michigan, I think, knew how to sweep dirt like a Indian I'll never know. Maybe it's natural. I don't think it's typical, though.

This one dude, older dude, they called Mr. C, was

walking around asking everybody if this stick of wood he was carrying belonged to them. He had this giant blue and orange thing coming off his nose, about *like* an orange, which it is why they called him Mr. C, I guess. A kid who was very pretty, built well—could of made a fortune in Montrose—ran to him with a bigger log and took him by the arm all the way back to his spot, some hanging builder's plastic and a chair, and set a fire for him. It's corny as hell, but I started liking the place. It was like a pilgrim place for pieces of shit, pieces of crud.

Then a couple gets me, tells me their life story if I'll drink instant coffee with them. The guy rescued the girl from some kind of mess in Arkansas that makes Tent City look like Paradise. He's about six-eight with mostly black teeth and sideburns growing into his mouth, and she's about four foot flat with a nice ass and all I can think of is how can they fuck and why would she let him. For some reason I asked him if he played basketball, and the *girl* pipes up, "*I* played basketball."

"Where?"

"In high school."

"Then what did you do?" I meant by this, how is it Yardog here has you and I don't.

"Nothing," she says.

"What do you mean, nothing?"

"I ain't done *nuttin*." That's the way she said it, too.

It was okay by me, but if she had fucked somebody other than the buzzard, it would have been *something*.

I was just kind of cruising there at this point, about like leg-up in Alvin, ready to buy them all a case of beer and talk about hard luck the way they wanted to, when something happened. This gleaming, purring, fully re-stored, *immaculate* as Brillo Tucker would say, '57 Chevy two-door pulls in and eases around Tent City and up to us, and out from behind the mirrored windshield, wear-ing sunglasses to match it, steps this nigger who was a kind of shiny, shoe-polish brown, and *exact* color and finish of the car. The next thing you saw was that his hair was black and oily and so were the black sidewalls of his car. Everything had dressing on it.

The nigger comes up all smiles and takes cards out of a special little pocket in his same brown suit as the car and himself. The card says something about com-munity development.

"I am prepared to offer all of you, if we have enough, a seminar in job-skills acquisition and full-employment methodology." This comes out of the gleaming nigger beside his purring '57 Chevy.

The girl with the nice butt who's done nothing but fuck a turkey vulture says, "Do what?"

Then the nigger starts on a roll about the seminar, about the only thing which in it people can catch is it will take six hours. That is longer than most of these people want to *hold* a job, including me at this point. I want to steal his car.

"Six hours?" the girl repeats. "For *what?*"

"Well, there are a lot of tricks to getting a job."

I say, "Like what?"

"Well, like shaking hands."

"Shaking hands." I remember Earl Campbell not buying my stinky shoes. That was okay. This is too far.

"Do you know how to shake hands?" the gleaming nigger asks. Out of the corner of my eye I see the turkey buzzard looking at his girl with a look that is like they're in high school and in love.

"Let's find out," I say. I grab him and crush him one, he winces.

"You know how to shake hands."

"I thought I did."

Who the fuck taught *him* how? Maybe Lyndon Johnson.

He purrs off to find a hall for the seminar, and the group at Tent City proposes putting a gas cylinder in the river and shooting it with a .22.

I've got my own brother to contend with, but we got over it a long time ago. He was long gone when ARMCO troubles let everybody else's brother loose on them. He, my brother, goes off to college, which I don't, which it pissed me off at the time, but not so much now. Anyway, he goes off and comes back with half-ass long hair talking *Russian*. Saying, *Goveryou po rooskie* in my face. It's about the time Earl Campbell has told me he won't wear my cleats because they stink, so I take all my brother's college crap laying down.

Then he says, "I study Russian with an old woman who escaped the Revolution with nothing. There's only one person in the class, so we meet at her house. Actually, we meet in her back yard, in a hole."

"You what?"

"We sit in a hole she dug and study Russian. All I lack being Dostoevsky's underground man is more time." He laughed.

"All I lack being a gigolo," I said, "is having a twelve-inch dick." And hit him, which is why he doesn't talk to me today, and I don't care. If he found out I was in the shower with my shotgun he'd pass in a box of shells. Underground man. What a piece of shit.

That's about it. Thinking of my brother, now, I don't feel so hot about running at the mouth. I'm not feeling so hot about living, so what? What call is it to drill people in their ear? I'm typical.

Letter from a Dogfighter's Aunt, Deceased

[***H**umpy, the stuck-up librarian, ruined little Brody.* There is a certain truth down in there allowing them a purchase, at least, upon what happened. For I must say that if I had not read so many books, I could only have seen Brody as a runaway and so would probably not have helped him. This is not to say, of course, that a more legitimate member of the family might not have come along, spotted him making his break, and helped him out of another motive: to teach him a lesson, let us say. His father would have done that, moral waste dump that he is.

Humpy'd turn over in her grave. They say that when a family member uses incorrect grammar—grammar so out of form, that is, that they, its chief torturers on earth, can recognize something awry. *Don't say ain't, your Aunt Humpy she'd turn over in her grave if she couldn't hardly hear you.* The remonstrated child, if he has some spirit, will sneak outside and put his mouth to the ground and yell *ain't* into the dirt, blowing ants and debris away from his dirty face. They have one of these, Brody's wife's sister's child, for whom I am performing unbid the services of guardian angel, endeared more and more to the little delinquent with each lip-to-ground utterance he calls me with.

What does happen in heaven—heaven or hell, it is purely a matter of choice, and I have ever preferred, no matter the situation, the happier name for it—what does happen when one is alleged to turn in a grave is generally that one does spin, but in a kind of spiritual pirouette. *Ain't, yestiddy, spose to,* and all precocious profanity comes shouted into the dirt and I do my tickled dance and love that child the more for daring to torture the dead.

You needn't believe me, but that—a high quotient of daring—is what heaven (again, call it hell if you will) is all about, if I may speak in earthly parlance. Here we are the children we were born as, without the myriad prejudices and passions and myopias that made us the human beings we mortally became. And when you can see, from the vantage of correct vision restored, a young child yet unoccupied by teachings human, it will make you dance. All guardian angels are secured in the first six days of human life.

This is a bit specious-looking for you. You do not want to buy it. You wonder, I hope you do, how I inform you of Brody's thoughts on picking damp bolls, the cruelty of having to pick damp cotton, the day he decided to run away. I tell you. Humpy, the dead egghead spinster librarian, tells you all they think and know on earth.

One night my special child, Lonnie, was involved in some ghost-story telling in a tent in the back yard. He went outside and squatted close and yelled *haint*. No one had corrected him against the word (or will); it was to him clearly guilty of association with *ain't*. Inches from his straining face a startled copperhead drew back. I possessed that snake to simply smile.

While it occurs to me, Brody did not become a dogfighter, any more than I was a queer librarian, despite his acknowledged associations with real dogfighters and despite my developed habit of looking over reading glasses at ill-bred men.

Here's Brody: I was going to be a *big dog*fighter. It's something. The *de*fenses. The *dogs* is still good. But . . . it's not for me. It's the people. The trash. It's just not for me.

His old man, the preacher: My boy, I don't know *what* he is, come specifically to it. I know he's *not* a preacher. I know he's got a hundred monsters on chains in a piece of swamp he bought. You tell me. I don't know what he is. What does a man do with monsters on chains in a swamp, comes by in a new Buick or new panel truck all the time? To talk about *nothing*. Any old kid can just trying things out run away once, even leave his own mother picking cotton alone—me, I was at the Bible convention. But to turn out a common man, that tries me, that almost tries my *faith*.

A dogfighter: Ho! Dogfight'll take ten *years* off your life. God, the yelling and swearing and . . . niggers! Nigger don't know how to act no matter *where* you put him. And they ain't all of it. I just go to cockfights now. *Gentlemen* still run a cockfight.

And dear Lonnie: My Aunt Humpy she is not buried very deep. She can hear talk. I think they don't even know where she is buried, because if you say certain things, anywhere, like even in Darlington under the canopy for a race, they say she can hear it even though you can't hear it yourself what your own self says. I want to be sure she hears it if she can get to turn over when she does.

My dear sister Cecelia: it's hard to say your own sister was a queer, but I have to admit it. That's the worst thing. Rescuing Brody from the brier patch with his tied-up suitcase was a drop in the bucket next to the main crimes, though that was about the first of the big ones. She was an intellectual. They say the library over at Pembert is still ahead of its time, even though they stopped spending money on it when she died. She had nothing to do with Brody *staying* gone four years, coming home married to a Mormon girl, of all things. They rolled up in a newish pickup, all sheepish looks at the ground, one sofa and about five of them dogs tied in the back, the dogs sitting on the sofa smiling at everything, like what a joke it all was.

Brody on the dogs: These dogs you read about eating babies don't have a thing to do with it. I've sold three thousand dogs in ten years and not one of them has bit a child or I'd know. I'd know about it *quick*, buddyro. I sell these dogs to people who pay $300, and when they pay $300 they don't expect something to eat their children. I don't think most of my dogs would bite a man without proper training, to tell the truth. They don't have to.

Ceece even says it: my picking up Brody and setting him on the road to ruin is minuscule. Queer. Ha. Or, Ho!

It is funny how folk can extrapolate aberrations ultimately all to the sexual: to say, the first child in a family of heathen to receive an education—to refine himself in virtually any way—will be sooner or later alleged homosexual. And naturally my relatives, my living relatives, were no different. Let me essay to classify us our clan directly, lest anyone waste energy on the very simplest of human taxonomy by my failure to state the obvious. We are white North Carolina Baptist—not the absolute worst run of trash on earth only because of a strange rubbing off of the otherwise bogus FIRST IN FREEDOM presumptions wafting out of the Research Triangle.

I am grateful to be able now to take the long view, as we say here. We see the earth many ways, time in its various dimensions—one of my favorites is the micrometer slice of a living life. It is possible to see Brody that day as if he is on a thin transparency cut from the waxen log that his whole life, and all lives around him, have come to be. The nice light of one pure moment shines easily through him as he stands, nervous, courage-screwed, hugging his suitcase, in the wet briers. He looks rather like an overgrown, beaten child. We can place a slice of a later Brody over this same setting: today, for example, he stands there waiting for me (not for me, for anyone) in blue polyester pants the color of the sky and an olive duck shirt he cannot keep tucked in, his crew cut a little shaggy, looking diffidently off to the ground near one of his hard shoes, still looking a little beat-up. That quality remains: though he did not become a dog-fighter, he did come close enough to share the common mark of the fraternity—the beaten-up. Dogfighters look, to a man (not to mention the ladies), beaten-up, despite brave cosmetics against it: buntline pistols, leather sport jackets, fancy boots, contractors' jewelry, full bellies and pomaded hair, and many, many Mickey Gilley smiles. This is partly why they take the pleasure they do in watching a thoroughbred dog, conditioned to a point suggesting piano wires and marble, reduced by another sculpted cat to a soft red lump resembling bloody terry cloth.

There is Brody, his nose suggesting a broken nose, his slightly wet eyes, looking mystified by nothing in particular, looking up the road at someone (me) coming, taking a deep breath to step out into view to discover if it is someone who will help or hinder him run away, to discover it is me and that he will need to compound the crime of escaping with that of lying. Yes'm, he says, almost before I ask, Ceece knows I'm going. Of course she knows.

Well, I guess she would, I say, smiling, touching his knee, which he has pressed hard into his suitcase, as though he would if he could compress the thing into nothing so that no more suspicion might be raised. This was the moment I first knew I was going to die. I do not mean to sound so melodramatic—I was to live yet for years.

I mean to say that when I saw Brody running, and when I saw myself aiding and abetting, I saw myself fully defined as the black sheep I was, and for once I was legitimate (I had *company*—with Brody there we were a conspiracy of two black-wool fools), and in a complex surge of emotion I loved little Brody, loved him much more than any queer aunt could confess, and I saw at the same time, as one truly does very few times in a normal life, that I was actually going to die someday, go to a funeral as the lead, and I considered seducing Brody and dismissed seducing Brody. He would hoot to hear that today, but *that* day he would not have chuckled, and I could have had my way with him, if a queer forty-year-old librarian popping out of a girdle did not scare the priapic wits out of him, which I presumed at the time not unlikely. And so I put Brody out on a corner in Lumberton, helped him become in his attempted escape the only other member of this clan to attend college (one of several accidents that befell him), and stand accused of—not merely accused, am held responsible for—his low living today, the very thing his escape was to have been from, and I the only one who helped him go.

Brody has come to ignore the church, crime one, and make money without holding a job, crime two. At this minute he is talking to a man he cannot understand in Taiwan who wants ten grown bulldogs. The Oriental cannot understand Brody either, because the English he knows is not the English Brody practices. And Brody is not altogether fluent in some Charlie Chan English that seems to parody the *r/l* problem.

Brody says: Imone sin you tin *young* dawgs.

Mr. Ho says: They rast rong time, we purchase rots burrdog to you, Mista Blode.

Brody: No sir, iss not the wrong time. I just caint keep puppies till they grown dawgs.

Ho: Rots.

Brody: Rots?

Ho: Yes!

Brody: What do you *mean*?

Ho: Satisfactly.

Brody: *What is*?

Ho: You, Mista Blode.

Brody: Send me a check for five thousand dollars.

Ho: Thank you.

———

How did Brody's escape fail? Or did it fail? Perhaps it did not. He came back with full intention of becoming a dogfighter. He fell, or stopped, short. He decided to make the dogs but not make them fight. Which is an inaccurately cute way of putting it: one doesn't need to make these dogs fight. They volunteer.

I couldn, you know, stand to knock so many dawgs in the head. That's what you have to do. He is talking about culling, culling the cowards and the inept from the brave and the strong, which in practice means shooting beautiful year-old dogs because they do not measure up. It is a point of pride with a dogfighter to allow a dog to *live* on his yard. This blood courage in dogs (parlance; I mean *in dogfighting*, but one commonly says *in dogs*) is an outrigger courage, a pontoon of vicarious guts running beside your own tipsy, slender, sinkable soul, your soul which accepts bad teeth, bad jobs, bad diet, which purports to refuse all injustice done you since and because of the Civil War, purports to accept no slight or slander and yet must take all and every, and so locates one accidental day, or night, a *dog*, two dogs with jaw muscles like golf balls addressing each other *like men*—not taking no for an answer. Your trod-down my-daddy's-daddy's-daddy-was-whipped-and-lost-his-cotton soul, now eating Cheetos instead of smothered quail and oysters hauled up from Charleston, standing there in blue jeans with a pistol in your armpit, sees an answer to all the daily failures of a failing late-trailer-payment life, and a dogfighter is born.

The real item: I tookeem home and tiedeem up in a inner tube and hungeem and beateem with a hammer. I coottn killeem acause he was swingin and bouncin like iss, springy—the rubber, you know, leteem git away. But

I gotteem, the quittin bastard, quit on me like that, I never been so embairsed in my life.

—If a dog fight for me an hour good as that—

—And you a fool, too.

—Well, tell you what, Jackie. Meet me ahine my house with your tube and your hammer, and I get me a rig, and we get up in a tree and go at it. I want to see *you* go an hour.

—You don't have the *least* notion what a good dog *is*.

—Yes I do. You had one.

—That's fuckin right. I had one. And I git rid of the next one I git like it the damned *straight* same way.

Alive, I never went to a dogfight, but I have been since. I did also go one night looking for Brody in his kennel, the first time I went there, and found myself suddenly ringed by what seemed large big cats axled to the ground on chains begging me with body wags to pet them.

His old man: If his Aunt Humpy had known what she was setting in motion that morning she'd of killed herself, I hope. We are not fancy people, airs and all, but we are not common. She might have even knowed he was lying, that Cecelia would of never let him go to Lumberton or anywhere else during cotton. But even so she could not have knowed that that little lift would have created our largest disgrace. It defies my logic. It defies my logic.

Brody: She wouldn't let it wait to dry out, and when you pull, you know, on the bolls, when they wet, they *pool* back, and you get this—it hurts.

My fine living relatives say that, in general, my

problem was reading too many books. What they cannot guess is that when I saw Brody step out of the briers on the Lumberton road I thought, There's Brody, making his move, as wild and plenary *as a character in a book.* I knew Ceece wasn't letting him go anywhere. He had on these huge, hard shoes and brilliant white socks, and he was pigeon-toed. His suitcase had straw on it. He even tried while standing to hide the suitcase between his legs, which made him more pigeon-toed.

I bought a beanfield, if fifty acres can be called a field, and Land Banked it, let it fallow, and took to walking the regenerating scrub in my after-work dress: pantsuit and parasol. For the first years I could be seen, of course, so the people were able to graft on one more badge of idiosyncrasy to the already highly decorated spinster librarian. The parasol contributed more to this, I think, than simply walking one's field (indeed, walking banked land out here is regarded a normal if unfortunate substitute for farming it), the parasol that carried with it—last seen bobbing over the tops of three-year pines— a suggestion of spinsterism that I believe included in local mythos not only elements Southern but New England as well. I was a kind of Scarlett-Emily, witch and Poppins, gathering beggar weeds. The truth was, I carried the umbrella less from a concern with image or sun than from a concern with lizards, of which I had an inordinate fear and an equally misinformed notion of parrying the assaults of with said rapier.

This field was a curious purchase for anyone, let alone a woman seen swordfighting lizards at dusk in it. It was worthless as cropland. But I had decided at some point to own some earth, and it did not matter to me which part, and that scrubby squat is what I took. Brody sweet himself put the idea in my head when he bought the adjacent fifteen acres that were even less desirable by farming standards. He got his dog stock chained down to it and managed thereby to depress even further the local values. So I took an adjacent fifty. You do things like that in life, and the less readily the act can be made to seem sensible the more gratifying it is. I was proud, daft owner of my useless spread, and in five years of strolling it I had intimate trails, trails pressed into the weeds by a combination of my random prowling and the more purposed prowling of rabbits and rodents and I think in the end even deer. I was happy with that sorry field.

I will confess to having lived finally a hungry, hollow life. I never left Pembroke and I had the stuff to have been anywhere. Yet whether my life was a failure or not is not the large matter, I hope: for I look at all the people who for one reason or another do not rise but remain routine and routinely small, and their failure as a class does not seem to amount to anything.

I took my pleasure then and now in small things— watching Brody run away one day, years later listening to him explain why he could not be a dogfighter, he there on the edge of his worthless plot and I on mine, his wild-eyed cat-dogs wagging at us. Brody excitedly telling me of his discovery of a new food concentrate that will save his money and his back, and of two puppies to be certified for international shipping—to Australia this time, where a man wants to see what they can do to kangaroos.

"Kangaroos?" I say. "Why hurt kangaroos?"

"I don't know, Humpy."

We must both have pictured our private, limited visions of kangaroo—gloved in carnivals, hopping the veld—and I remember thinking this is life, my life, standing at dusk speculating about the fate of a dimly known marsupial with my dimly known nephew I once rescued from pulling damp bolls and maybe from more, and Brody no doubt was thinking a bit less heavily, with refreshingly less profundity, about sending the *red-and-white male or the larger washed-out gray dog, who might do better,* against the down-under foe he's heard can disembowel a man.

"Good night, Brody."

" 'Night, Humpy."

He stands there a minute more, as I do, he in his slippery, hard dress shoes, which he perversely insists on wearing instead of practical boots. He is yet escaping that original, damp field, dressed for travel. The moon glints off these large, shiny wingtips, which trod uncertain across the sloping dirt to the jumping dogs.

Mr. Irony

[I am a student of low-affect living edged with self-deprecating irony.

I am a character of lower-affect living a bit on edge with Mr. Irony, a self-deprecating therapist.

A therapist of self-deprecation, teaching the presumptuous among us to edge ourselves with irony until we can be said to be low-affect burghers of the modern world, appropriate denizens of the modern world, Mr. Irony sits on the edge of the sofa smoking with his leg crossed over his knee after the fashion of a lady crossing her leg over her knee, not after the fashion of a man crossing his, etc., a manly configuration suggesting, from above at least, more the figure 4 than Mr. Irony's position does. Mr. Irony's position—smoking and bouncing his shoe in front of him, in the air in front of him, his shoe edged with the black trim applied by the black man at the barber shop with a toothbrush—suggests a pair of scissors more than a figure 4. His legs cut in slight snips the airy fabric of irony in the apartment around us.

Mr. Irony cuts a pattern of ironic air into certain pieces; they assemble on the carpet in no real order, to be sewn later into a garment, a coat of irony perhaps, a just-reminiscent-of-Nehru shirt-jac not for sale in any but the most hip low-affect haberdasheries in the world. This coat Mr. Irony will edge with a piping of flamingo pink he has begun to remove absently from the sofa upon which he scissors.

I will be expected to wear the ironic shirt-jac edged with flamingo piping as part of my low-affect therapy unless I do something. Doing something is precisely against the grain of Mr. Irony's teaching, and yet if I were not resistant to becoming a low-affect self-deprecating character I would not need Mr. Irony to instruct me, and he is of course fully aware that pulling the piping for the jacket for me to wear in consummate humiliation—no. He is not aware, not aware that I am nervous about wearing the ironic coat. I must get Mr. Irony some wine, white wine, to occupy his hand that absently pulls the piping for the jacket. I shall tape the piping back into place. A ridiculous restoration that will crackle and fail, crackle and make Mr. Irony notice it with a particular, subtle smile. Then he will be aware.

He will be amused, tolerant of my device to not yet have to wear a late-Nehru jacket with flamingo edging in the irony-edged world. In my device to forestall the dismantling of the sofa he will see the natural Young Republican resistance to self-deprecating irony-edged low-affect living, and it will confirm his presence as my roommate and tutor, and he will scissor some more air, touch lightly the tape I've transparently tried to stop him with, sip his wine, think well of me. He has a good student who ever questions the development he seeks, a resistant student all the more worthy, for that resistance, of his efforts, and valuable to him, as are heathen to their converters for their very backwardness; a student who will come round, come round, come round in a swoon of faithful self-deprecation into the low-affect irony-feathered dance of life, the limbo of bending backwards so far that no disappointment can get beneath you, no rug of unexpected loss, jerked, can ever surprise. "Things do not turn out well," Mr. Irony says.

"May I get you more wine?"

"More wine."

"More wine, sir."

"My man."

"May we look out the window at joggers, sir?"

"Fine plan."

Mr. Irony and I go out, for a lesson, to look at alligators. The alligators, located easily, display themselves, as if for our benefit, by walking about high-legged, out of the water, like dogs. "The crocodilian," Mr. Irony says, "the crocodilian is not a creature of irony." When Mr. Irony says *irony*, which he seldom does, he undergoes a phenomenon of nature, or of supernature: his edges recede and expand, almost at once, as if he *italicizes*. "The shark, by contrast, is a creature of irony." Again he shimmers, he *thins*, is momentarily less and more than he was as he spoke the words "The shark, by contrast, is a creature of." "In the gut of the shark you will find the license plate of the auto, the leg of the mannequin. Not so the gut of *Alligator mississippiensis*. In there," he goes on, "at best the golf ball, the turtle." The field trip is concluded.

All incidents roll off Mr. Irony's mind like a drop of the water of dailiness from the oiled back of the duck of time. Mr. Irony has taught me locutions like this.

"Just to try," he says. "To hone. To play. To discover."

"Mr. Irony."

"Yes?"

"Why? What does saying the oiled back of the duck of time exactly *do*—I mean, do for me as someone—"

"As someone seeking to edge himself with irony, put a self-deprecating piping around his minimal self-importance?"

"Yes, how does the playful locution do this?"

Mr. Irony will look at me over his glasses, a gesture I have come to know means that he disapproves of my questioning so bluntly; he is looking to see if perhaps I am not joking, hedging us up with feigned obtuseness. But no, I am not: I am obtuse.

"*The oiled back of the duck of time* does not precisely itself *do anything*. Whence it wends our way?"

"Well, I said it, or thought it."

"You can make money and be famous if you *write* what you say or think, and the difference is therefore enormous."

"Yes, sir. I wrote that incidents fall from your mind as drops of daily water from the duckback of time."

"Not bad, that. You changed it somewhat."

"Thank you, sir."

———

I invited Mr. Irony on a trip around the world. "I'm sure you've been, of course," I said.

"Be less sure," he said.

"What's that mean, sir?"

"Means, mostly."

"You don't care to go, then?"

"Didn't say that."

Mr. Irony was irritable. I leveled his glass with wine from the coldest part of the refrigerator. The colder, the less likely he is to deem it vinegar. I considered dropping the subject of world touring until he perked up. All subjects except perking up, in fact, and that subject never to be broached. The coldness of the wine made Mr. Irony open his mouth and extend his head forward as if he were a goose about to honk.

"For two?"

"Excuse me?"

"You spoke of taking Magellan's cruise, I believe. *For two?*"

"Yes, sir. Unless—"

"—?"

"I could get more tickets: $1.50 each."

"Most reasonable. Do tell."

"Pulled them from *Duke*, sir. Man at His Best just reads the travel section, and these, perforated in the binding, are his world-tour tickets, sir. Two tickets, $3.00 magazine. Man at His Best."

"You said that. Play a joke, as a ball in golf, *once.*"

"Yes, sir."

Mr. Irony sat regarding this proposition in the attitude of one regarding no proposition at all. This was part of the method, and I confess there may be more to it. It is possible Mr. Irony was regarding the proposition with his entire being, or with 10 percent, while the other 90 percent was regarding all the things tangential to talking with a student. *Optic yellow tennis balls* might well have been at the center of his brain.

"Not easy to do, I know," he said, apparently referring to the golf-ball conceit, and, if so, demonstrating a rare instance of tutorial sympathy. I took advantage of the soft-looking moment.

"Do you care to go or *not*, sir?"

"Care to go."

"More tickets, then?"

"Two more'd be nice."

"For your wife, sir, and—"

"Not my wife. Not my wife. And not my wife."

"Anyone *in* mind, sir?"

"Not yet. What is the mode of travel?"

"Varies, sir."

"—?"

"Unspecified, sir. On the ticket: *unspecified variable means of transport.*"

"Makes one rather reconsider the wife," he said, scissoring his leg. He was feeling considerably better. "Short of planes that land too hard, nothing more pleasing to me, less to the wife, than transportation that doesn't work."

"Minimizes the self-importance of the individual, sir?"

"*Naturalmente.*"

"You'd best," Mr. Irony said before we purchased our extra tickets, "you'd best make sure that *Duke* allows Men at Their Best to travel with women."

"Right," I said. He had a point.

I checked the matter. The woman I spoke with at *Duke* assured me that the $1.50 world-tour ticket would be honored without respect to sex. I got us another two tickets, and Mr. Irony and I went down to the International Hostelry for Available Traveling Women.

At the International Hostelry for Available Traveling Women we were abruptly led to a gymnasium filled with cots and women. We were received, on the floor, not unlike visitors to a dog pound. A few women remained still, a few showed us minor interest, but most jumped up and wagged themselves violently at us. "I've seen this spectrum of behavior in a whorehouse in Texas," Mr. Irony remarked, not ostensibly looking at any of the women.

Out of a sense of courtesy, I looked at the women. They were, most of them, beautiful. I felt, in fact, as if I were drowning before a replay of all the missed sexual opportunities of a lifetime.

"Gravid with heat in here," Mr. Irony said.

"Yessir."

Some of the women leapt up, approached us; others held back, deliberately diverting themselves; others remained indifferent. "Flat on their backs, those two," Mr. Irony pointed out, indicating in a corner two supine figures on cots. Beneath their cots, packed backpacks: two neat bundles, in distinct contrast to the sloppy, strewn, dorm-room environs of the cheerier, aggressive women.

"Be polite among Harpy as I steer us to the Defeated Ones," Mr. Irony instructed. This I did, occasionally shaking hands, as Mr. Irony tugboated us to the corner of the absolute uninterest.

We stood between the two cots looking at two broad-hipped women in cotton shirts. They were similar enough to be sisters: square faces, full lips, wide eyes.

"You girls healthy?" Mr. Irony asked.

"I'm as fine as frogs' hair and she's right as rain," one of them said, motionless.

"Be down," said Mr. Irony. "Do you cost more, or come with liabilities, or strings, or whatever, for this sour demeanor which wins a sane man?"

The woman who had spoken looked at her companion.

"No," the companion said.

" 'Tis settled, then," Mr. Irony said. "We court you." He turned to me. "This would be my opinion *extempore* regarding world-traveling companions. You have a voice in the matter."

"Mr. Irony," I said, pulling him a bit out of earshot, "ordinarily I would hesitate to differ, would automatically defer to your experience. But I confess to have wanted twenty women in here more than these. *But*. Now I'm won. These are the girls one finds in a suburban cowboy club, looking for love. They are of good stock, well-bred, well-heeled in the moral zone but not without appetites one could call—"

"It's wonderful you are filled with ideas, son. Keep them to yourself."

Mr. Irony turned to the women. "Ladies, a world tour?"

They hit the floor, boots on.

We made arrangements to meet them later. On the way out, Mr. Irony turned to me and said, "Unless I miss my mark, these girls don't expect things to turn out well. My kind."

"They'd better not," I said.

This was the sort of obtrusive remark Mr. Irony

ignores. I was having more and more trouble getting in a word edgewise. It was making me sullen rather than ironic.

First stop, on the cliffs of Acapulco, the girls stand, nipples spiked up in the salty breeze, as Mr. Irony prepares to make the 85-foot dive into the swells. "One of the more challenging stretches of your *Duke* world tour," our *Duke* brochure tells us.

"If he can do it," my Traveling Woman says, "I can do it, and I can do it *nekkid*."

Mr. Irony takes deep breaths. I read to him from the brochure: "You must determine the seventh and largest swell of the series and count to seven once it clears the large rock on the left. Don't look back, and keep it tight."

"That it?"

"That's it, sir."

"And grap your *cojones, señor*," a local boy adds, watching the spectacle of gringos with considerable excitation. Mr. Irony grabs himself, with two hands, before tumbling from the cliff in a spidery roll altogether suggestive of a horse taking a fall.

From the swell into which he exploded, we see Mr. Irony's red face surface, unquestionably smiling. The word *real* wafts to us, in reverb, seconds after we see his mouth open and close.

"Shit," my Traveling Woman says. "The turkey survived."

"Grap your teeties," the boy tells her.

Atop elephants in Lanxang, we hear Mr. Irony say, "I am immortal. I have died a thousand deaths." I turn to acknowledge that I am all ears. "Of the imagination," he says, as we lurch over this small but important part of the world.

Each of us has grown accustomed to the odor of the elephant he rides but not to that of the mahout behind whom he sits. The Traveling Women, on the third and fourth elephants, have complained of this very thing.

"Deodorant would go a long way here," a Traveling Woman said.

"Or nowhere," the other Traveling Woman said.

Mr. Irony, in the lead, then approved of this sentiment with a pursing of his lips barely noticeable before his face filled with rare emotion, in time with the stepping of his elephant into a stream from the bank of which could be seen sliding crocodiles, or something that looked like crocodiles. I was given the lead, following the fording.

Lanxang is small but important because it is contiguous to—a bridge connecting, therefore—two other small and likewise important places of the earth. The smaller the place, we have come to note on this tour, the more important. "What is a continent but spoonfuls of dirt?" Mr. Irony asked, early on, before the rest of us had arrived at this logic.

"Oh brother," one of the Traveling Women said. She became with that remark not Mr. Irony's but my Traveling Woman.

"Indulgences!" Mr. Irony proclaimed, his call to order for word jazz. He slapped his elephant's hide. "The head of my animal is a small V-8 engine covered by slab bacon."

"Fatback."

"Fatback with hairs."

"A hemi. A flat-head. Not a V-8."

"Who said that?" Mr. Irony asked. "The girl from Pampa or the girl from Borger?"

"The girl from Borger," the girl from Pampa said. "Her daddy raced."

"Flat-head has some merit, indeed."

"Gray twelve-gauge Naugahyde," the girl from Pampa said.

"Fatback, gray-brown, boar-bristled, flat-head six underneath," said Mr. Irony.

"Never forgetting," said Pampa.

"An elephant's timing chain of memory never breaks," said Borger.

"We are astride some fine beast."

I don't indulge. I am beginning to doubt the wisdom of my appointment to Mr. Irony.

The tent was filled with censers and their various sweet smokes, and we were sitting foursquare to a hookah in the middle.

Someone, holding breath, said, "What kind dope?"

Someone else, holding, shrugging, said, " 'on't know."

"Man at His Best," Mr. Irony intoned, "asks not what specie of intoxicant his hosts provide." Then he addressed the girl from Pampa. "Her daddy raced. What yours?"

"My daddy sat on his Texass in a Barcalounger size of a Lincoln." She pulled on the hookah. Mr. Irony studied her. With her lungs at full expansion, letting no smoke escape, she said: "Come I know Naugahyde."

In relation to elephants, to the canvas and skins around us and under us, Naugahyde was a mysterious thing to think about just then, and Mr. Irony accordingly announced "Indulgences!" and slapped a provision crate with sufficient speed and force that everyone exhaled, losing smoke.

Spontaneously, my girl from Pampa indulged: "He was a lardass from the gitgo. Had all he ever wanted, so all he wanted was to git rid of that and git shit he didn't want. We had land, oil, stock, and three TV's in a wall-bank, like Elvis and Lyndon. The recliner had motors in it like a hospital bed—drive it around, too. Vibrated, heated up, everything. Air brakes. It came in leather. Then he heard about Naugahyde. Had to have it. Drove the lounger down to the upohster's, rip rap."

"One is cautioned by all sense against becoming fond of an Available Traveling Woman," Mr. Irony said. "Damned if the temptation does not accrue."

"Who?" his girl from Borger said. "Her? Shoot. She's a card. I coulda tole y'all that."

"Had a *refrigerator* in it, under his ass."

We started laughing then, unstoppable dope laughter, fueled on knowing there's nothing so finally funny enough to cause such paroxysms. *To the upohster's,* someone kept repeating as we came up for air, sending us back under again. We were prostrate in a tent carpeted of animal hides, noses in fur, thinking of Naugahyde, unable to breathe.

At Jack London's Trading Post and Juice Bar/Trail Foods, Inc., we outfit for a brief walk on what *Duke* details as "the tundra."

"The parka with raglan sleeves for me, I favor Lord Raglan," Mr. Irony tells a clerk. "Anoraks for the ano-rectics," he says, with an impatient wave at the Traveling

Women, who ignore him. They are feeling the goods: the down-filled, the corduroy, the leather, siliconed, mink-oiled.

Dressed out, fat as bales of cotton, we look not unlike designer astronauts, and we clod into the Juice Bar, where we all four enjoy White Fang Smoothies before stepping out on the tundra.

"Tundra? I've led *cheers* on ground worse'n this," a Traveling Woman says. "In Pampa."

"Just enough bad ground to scuff up our moon boots, ladies," Mr. Irony says. "That's the objective here, I daresay. Man at His Best not to be seen in new shoes."

Riding a Galápagos tortoise, Mr. Irony says, "I do not recall ever feeling so at home."

The tortoise's head, high up, looks not altogether different from Mr. Irony's head, which is only a bit larger and a little higher than the reptile's. Mr. Irony's knees are up also, his cowboy boots in carved notches of the carapace.

"It seems to me all we do on this *Duke* tour is ride things, jump off things, slip and bust our ass on things," one of the Traveling Women says.

"Man at His Best," the other offers.

"Komodo dragons next, ladies. Flesh-eaters," Mr. Irony says. They do not respond. They have read ahead the literature and know that we are scheduled to ride no dragons. Next we dance in grass skirts before tourists drinking drinks from coconut shells, dance across an atoll.

Mr. Irony's reptilian steed stops to graze on what looks like a small cabbage. Mr. Irony sits sidesaddle, lights a cigarette. "These old boys know what they are about.

I would not presume to hurry the duocentenarian." The tortoise eats with surprising waste, cabbage bits at times even on top of his head. "It is possible," Mr. Irony says, watching him scatter his meal, "to hazard another end for the dinosaur: inefficient table dexterity."

"I shall inquire if one is permitted to own for himself so measured a hedon," Mr. Irony says. "I shall walk him in Central Park, *at night*."

"Mr. Irony, what is your position on the Good Ole Days?"

"What you mean?"

"I get the notion, from no particular event, that when one is correctly minimalized and hedged up with self-deprecating irony, et cetera, that one doesn't—can't, by definition—afford to care about the Good Ole Days."

"I don't understand you," Mr. Irony says.

I take this for an evasion. I am on to something but I have asked it too directly—I have asked it *at all*.

This whole business of his sitting with such fondness on a two-hundred-year-old turtle is a way, as I see it, of disowning a more recent time, a time, say, of tricycle-sitting sullied somehow by a dominating father; a time after which boyish enthusiasms became adolescent agonies became adultish early losses and defeats, leading Mr. Irony to the defensive position of assuming that things don't turn out well. Sitting astride a dinosaur confirms him, proves in a tacit, cabbage-bashing fashion that the Good Ole Days are the fluff of myth. The truth for Mr. Irony is extinction, a brief run through the ironic daily maze and not dying *yet*. On his tortoise, Mr. Irony looks as composed and serene as an underfed Buddha.

"You been having both the women?" he suddenly asks.

"Sir! Both got in my tent, both—well, pleasured. But the seed only in one."

"Still, you put your trocar in mine, too."

"Yes, sir. It's—"

"Understandable. My fault. I shall seek to win back my Available Traveling Woman shortly."

"Good, sir. I—"

"Shut up."

For three days we live in enamel tubs, under steamed towels, on massage tables, in Hot Springs, Ark.

"This is geezerhood, but it's nice, but it's still geezerhood," the Borger Traveling Woman says. After the second day, Pampa says, "I feel like a grub."

Mr. Irony has acquired a laboratory wash bottle, one liter Nalgene, which he fills with vodka before a day in the baths, and when an attendant instructs him to drink the hot spring water ("to warm your *insides*") from a proffered folding paper cup, Mr. Irony produces from the tub of 110-degree water in which he reposes the wash bottle—he smiles and squirts a stream of hot vodka in, nodding the attendant away.

"Nice rig," Borger comments.

"Germ-free," Mr. Irony instructs.

Mr. Irony does not attain the parboiled look we three have, and his step is sharp, his stride long. The rest of us, mineralized and boiled and sober, veer along softly.

"Now I feel like one of those catfish that live in caves," Pampa says after the third and final day in steam.

"The white ones, dear?" Mr. Irony asks.

"White, *blind* ones, *dear*." She looks around, suspicious of Mr. Irony's term of affection. The Traveling

Women share a low-lidded squint with one another. *Something fishy.*

In a bar across from the grand row of baths, Mr. Irony declares that he will help us. "I propose to restore you to your electrolytical feet. Allow me." He orders a pitcher of vodka and three ponies of liqueurs for us each. "Sup at these as you would side dishes. This," Mr. Irony says, lifting the pitcher, "is the roast beef."

In fifteen minutes we are well along onto our electrolytical feet. The Traveling Women are crying with affection for Mr. Irony, hugging him, and I cannot shake the sensation that I am an eel. Mr. Irony tenders a speech. "Ladies, forgive me my earlier curtnesses with you. I meant no harm. Sexism is, if you will, etiological."

"Do what?"

"A long time ago," Mr. Irony says, "a crocodile bit a hippopotamus on the nose and effected, *voilà*"—Mr. Irony touches his nose and slides his arm away from him into space, trombone style—"an elephant."

The Traveling Women enjoy a look of profound eye-widening comprehension. "And elephants *don't forget,*" they say, nearly in unison.

"Precisely. And I am sorry," Mr. Irony says, bowing his head. With tears the Traveling Women look at him, and they hug each other.

"Mr. Irony," I manage to say, "were the liquid in me not absorbed into cottony cells, had I fodder at all, sir, if I felt like anything but a starved moray eel, I'd throw up."

"Hedge up, boy. Minimalize your self-importance. Limn with humility."

"Rock breaks scissors," I say, feeling my way, speaking automatically. "Scissors cut paper. Paper covers rock. Poon breaks irony."

Mr. Irony purses his lips, looks at the end of his cigarette, as if waiting for my tirade to end. "Not bad. Keep it to yourself."

"Mr. Irony, have you been bitten hard?"

"Elucidate."

"The—the Ingenue thing. There are, apparently, life's Ingenues and life's Vietnam Boys, and—"

"The inconsequential and the consequential?"

"Yes, sir. The bitten-hard."

"The bitten-hard. I see now. I see."

We are in hot-air balloons, jetting on a blue plume activated by a pull cord over desert. Mr. Irony watches the ground carefully to spot something at which a ballast bag might be thrown. "I would not counsel your courting the hard bite," he says. "Is that a shack?"

"Looks like it, sir."

"Bombs away." The flour sack speeds in a miraculous arc down to the tin roof of the shack and strikes with a sound not unlike a child striking an oatmeal box. "Gabby Hayes should dash out in a state of confusion, precisely *now*," Mr. Irony says. As we drift away, no one emerges from the shack. "He consumed—that prospector—too much red-eye last night." We are in a silent, unfired drift, only the creaking of the basket to be heard.

"I have the feeling," I say, "that there are hard-bitten folk walking around with a certain advantage over those of us who haven't had . . . well—"

"Do people with one arm have a certain advantage over those with two? Yes, in a way: they know something unstandard. Same for the bitten brain, the psychological one-arm. But, son, listen: irony will not survive the bite, the truly hard bite."

Mr. Irony shimmers at the word, perhaps more clearly than I've seen him shimmer before, because, I think at the time, of the clear desert air and our altitude.

Mr. Irony hefts up another bag. "You may be silly, on the one hand, or wounded, on the other, but you do not *elect* to be wounded. Is that a dune buggy?"

"Yes, sir."

"Helmets on 'em?"

"Looks to be, sir."

"Your shot."

I let the bag go and it hits the desert in a broadening white puff.

"Missed by a quarter mile, I'd say," Mr. Irony assesses.

"It's a moving target, sir."

"And from a moving gun."

"It's the girls, I think."

"Hand me a bag."

Following a column of mountain goats, Mr. Irony, angular and bearded, looks not unlike a common goat chasing its betters.

"We'll never shoot one of them things," Pampa says.

"We're not supposed to," Mr. Irony impatiently declares, sighing, stepping carefully up the rocks. "We're supposed to tire and drop our rifles from fatigue and descend to the lodge with our blisters." There are tiny radio transmitters on the rifles which would seem to corroborate Mr. Irony's assessment of what we're to do on *Duke*'s Man-at-His-Best Rocky Mountain Goat Safari.

There's a curious footnote in the brochure: "If hunters wish, they may, as in recent American combat experience, jettison their weapons."

"Thing to do," Mr. Irony says, "is put these damned cannon someplace they can't get to with the helicopter—make 'em hike in."

"Chap some ass," Borger says.

"Chap some ass," Pampa adds.

"Chap some ass," Mr. Irony says.

As the goats continue to move vertically, their powerful bushy rumps just out of range, we turn laterally and head for a close-looking space between two peaks. Mr. Irony says: "Mine shaft'd be nice."

We were given the opportunity to choose means of transport during the next leg of *Duke*'s Man-at-His-Best World Tour. The territory to be crossed was Georgia and South Carolina, south to north. We could take I-95 with a life-insurance salesman who had once been an oil rigger and then had tried to be a bass guide for Roland Martin, or we could take back roads in a log truck with a crew of pulpwooders. *Duke* said, "Excuse the indelicacy, but in local parlance these fellows, black or white, are known as pulpwood niggers, and they stink to high heaven, have potted meat and Mellow Yellow for lunch, do not visit dentists." There was no question which Mr. Irony would choose, and we were not surprised to see Borger and Pampa pile into the insurance salesman/bass guide's 4 × 4 Blazer Silverado with smoked glass all around. As the doors closed, we saw the salesman spray a shot of Binaca into his mouth.

"His hairdo was not unreminiscent, was it, of Woody Woodpecker?" Mr. Irony asked.

"I thought so myself," I said, and I had, precisely. The coiffure looked artificially blown up, almost teased, into a topknot at the front of the fellow's head, and it was in fact carrot-colored. Mr. Irony and I, by this sight, were reassured that we had made the correct choice of transport. We sat together on the cooler of beer *Duke* had advised us to prepare for our ride with the pulp-wood niggers, patient in our waiting, for *Duke* had also advised that, though we would arrive at the destination (Dillon, S.C.) well before the insurance salesman would have gotten us there, we might depart up to two hours later.

The pulpwood niggers were three. The driver was white, wearing a blue mesh cap that read *I'm a Rebel and Damn* PROUD OF IT. At shotgun was a black with his hair plaited into spikes, over which he had tied a black nylon scarf in Arab fashion, with two nylon tails down his back. "Healthy-looking individual," Mr. Irony remarked of him. "Got them Husqvarna arms." In the middle of the seat was a suggestion of human form, as a cicada hull on a pine tree suggests an insect. He was chinless, chestless, slumped down bleary-eyed between his larger colleagues. We came to learn he was "the oiler," by which title was signified his entire *raison d'être*: when the other two ran equipment, he carried and administered the lubricants. If it was chain saws, he carried a pistol-style oil can, squirting the hot blades, muttering every time, "Self-oilers don't work *for shit*."

The driver, with a motion of his thumb, indicated we were to get on the truck flatbed. We got aboard and were arranging ourselves on the boat cushions we bought with the cooler when the cab rear window slid open and the oiler extended both arms through it. Mr. Irony and I managed to interpret this, and I handed the oiler two cold beers.

"Fatherlaw died last week," he said, pulling back into the cab with the beer. With a jolt we were off.

Several miles down the road his arms came back through the window, and he was delivered two more beers. "Wife daddy died," he said, going back in.

Through a rare, obvious communion, Mr. Irony and I were clearly taking extreme pleasure in the ludicrousness of our scene, glancing squarely and without expression at one another during these utterances from the oiler. We were bouncing clear off the truck, on a clay road that now had over it behind us a cloud of dust as far as we could see.

We braked to a halt, and while Mr. Irony and I were still struggling for balance, the driver and the black guy were pissing in the road beside open cab doors. "Pit stop," the oiler informed us, a bit gratuitously. We got off to piss.

Mr. Irony was boring into the clay in front of him when the black dude said to him, "Nice boots, homeboy."

"Thank you, sir."

"Pointy-like. Match your head."

"They do, sir."

"Spensive, bet. How much they coss, homeboy?"

"Three."

The oiler interrupted this discourse by letting himself out of the truck and collapsing on the roadside.

"*Lumpydaddydied!*" he said, rocking on the ground like a child in a crib. Mr. Irony bent to inspect the bereaved form.

"Pay no mine, homeboy," the black said to Mr. Irony. "He in moning. Would like them boots."

"For the asking, sir." Mr. Irony was already seated on the truck bed pulling hard on one of his Luccheses. It was this willingness, this anticipation, I think, that saved Mr. Irony's boots. The black looked with just a hint of surprise at Mr. Irony sitting unshod, swinging his socked feet.

"I just try 'em on, homeboy. You all right."

"Might I kick a few clods in those brogans?"

"Righteous. You bit crazy."

The two of them exchanged footwear, and the black walked awkwardly around, stopping with the boots under the prostrate, grieving face of the oiler.

"How these look on me, Taint?"

"Leave him alone, Rooster," the driver said. "Pick him up." He was smoking, leaning against the truck studying his calloused hands.

"How they look, Taint?" Rooster repeated.

"Lumpy daddy *died*."

Rooster leaned over, off balance, and with one arm picked the oiler up, setting him down on his feet hard, giving him the slightest steadying shake. "Get hole on yourself, man." The oiler suddenly reminded me of a creature I saw once in an aquarium that I thought merely remained still for a very long time and that I later discovered to have been all along dead, hollowed out.

The driver flicked his cigarette into the woods and got in the truck. "That fag magazine don't pay us *shit* for this *shit*. You boys get on."

Mr. Irony, who had been speaking with Rooster, unhooked the boom cable and Rooster released the winch. Mr. Irony pulled ten feet of cable out and got aboard with it. "Homeboy want him a seat belt," Rooster said, to no one. He stuffed the oiler in the rider's door. "Homeboy I think may be hisself part nigger. Here. Peench like motherfuck anyway." Mr. Irony's Luccheses came through the rear window, and Rooster's brogans, loaded with beer, went in.

Mr. Irony put two half hitches of cable around his waist and looked to me with a gesture offering some cable, which I declined. He took another half hitch for himself and we settled in, looking backwards, for the ride to Dillon.

Once we had a head of steam and the dust trail behind us well up, Rooster's arm came through the window and touched the winch control. Mr. Irony put two beers in his jacket, felt his waist, took a deep breath, gave Rooster a thumbs-up, and Rooster winched him free of the bed. He swung out and back, spinning, and settled bed-high beneath the log boom, blowing, turning, already taking on the color of clay, assuming the orientations of a sky diver, the expression on his face rapt.

Just before he disappeared for good into the thick clay air, Mr. Irony managed to face forward, horizontal, with arms out front, and shout, "*Super*man at His Best!"

"Life insurance is the best investment money can buy. You are investing *in your life*—and what could be a better investment than that? *What?*"

"Don't you have to *die* to cash in?"

"Alack! No, ladies. That's a thing I read in a Shakespeare story. Nooo, ladies, you do not have to die to enjoy the extreme uncomparable benefits of cash-value life insurance. You may borrow against your policy, and it may mature and pay *before* you die, and—"

"What's this?"

"What?"

"It says, ODOR KILLER—CITRUS. AN ENTIRE ORANGE GROVE IN A BOTTLE. "

"Hey! Don't squirt too much of that!"

"Open the windows, for God's sake."

"Entire orange grove in an entire goddamn car."

"Well, I told you—"

"What's *this*? It *stinks*." Pampa sniffs a cardboard coaster suspended from the rearview mirror; on the coaster is a painting of a largemouth bass.

"Air freshener," the life insurance salesman says.

"*Fish* air freshener?"

"Well, no. It's—"

"Here's some Eau de Paris—NOIR."

"*That's* expensive."

"Oh!"

"Windows! Stop that shit, Borger," Pampa says.

"What *is* all this crap?" Borger asks.

"Yeah. Are we in the presence of a *complex* here?"

"No, I just like to keep my car spotless. I live in this car—work in this car fifteen-sixteen hours a day."

"Well, it doesn't have to smell like a whorehouse."

"Well—you know how sometimes a car just gets an odor in it that . . . doesn't go away?"

"*No*," Pampa says.

"*No*," Borger says.

"You know, kind of *under* things?"

"*No.*"

"No. God. Did he *fart*?"

"Heysoos. I get the picture. Spot of ORANGE GROVE up here, Borger."

A stop is made for urination all around. Mr. Irony, whose clay-caked face resembles a terra-cotta mask, declines to unwinch and pees from the Superman position.

"Look, Mom, no hands," he says.

Rooster says to me, "That is one *trazy* white man."

The oiler heads for the ditch in a mincing wobble and appears to start to wilt when Rooster suspends him by the back of the shirt. "And he *still* dead, Taint," Rooster whispers to him, shoving him back toward the truck. "Pitiful. Pitt-ee-full."

"Load my bomb bays, kind sirs," Mr. Irony calls.

Responding as to a regular call for workaday lubrication, the oiler pulls himself to with a big sniff and hurries to Mr. Irony with two more cold beers, which Mr. Irony instructs him to slip into the pockets of his jacket.

"You will surmount your troubles, son," Mr. Irony says to him. "Your wife's father died and he will remain dead, as Mr. Rooster has so sagely informed you. The world means you no harm. Be brave, be brave, and be strong." Mr. Irony makes a gesture in the air that suggests a blessing and that throws him out of the Superman orientation, and we fire up and are off in a scratch of rock and rubber and clay, Mr. Irony in a spinning circle-within-a-circle boomerang motion.

"Well, thing is, see, she's a young girl—big girl, you girls would like her, being as you're from Texas and all, fine state, did my time out there yessiree on rigs outside Odessa, nice folk, hospitality-wise—she's young,

Debbie, and absolutely in love w'me, see—she's never been that before so she's, like, skeptical."

"We trust you encourage her in that skepticism," Borger says.

"Hey, what's that supposed to mean?"

"There they are," Pampa says.

In the parking lot of a boarded-up convenience store in the center of Dillon, S.C., is the log truck, and drinking beer are the blue-Rebel-capped driver, the crumbling oiler laughing with his head thrown back, Rooster, the student of low-affect living edged with self-deprecating irony, and, suspended yet from the boom, orange as a kapok life jacket head-to-toe, Mr. Irony himself.

"Is that your not-husband?" Pampa asks Borger.

"Goose by any other name," Borger says.

"Hey. What's the deal? That's a *dude*?" the insurance salesman asks.

"That's a dude, mister."

"Hey. *All right*. He looks like I could sell him some life insurance, you think? What you think? Worth a try or not or what!"

The life insurance salesman gets out of the smoked-glass Blazer and shakes down his pants legs over his Italian ankle boots and walks in a confident stride for Mr. Irony. Before he reaches him, Borger rushes to the orange horizontal figure with the hurried pumping vigor of a sailor's wife greeting her sailor after six months at sea, and she kisses the unbooted end of it fully upon its clay-caked crusty terra-cotta lips and says, "Oh, honey, you smell *good*!" and the life insurance salesman turns on his heel and retreats, his face a configuration of pure confusion.

———

Swatting handfuls of the thick, nearly leavened clay dust from himself in a three-quarter beat, Mr. Irony said, to the beat, in time, "Dark, dark candy; light, light pain; green, green fruit; trying, trying times."

"Is that a quote?" the driver asked.

"Yeah, I've heard that somewhere," the insurance salesman said. "Maybe Shakespeare."

"Do I detect shower stalls across the boulevard?" Across the street was a coin-operated car wash, to which Mr. Irony made a straight path, removing his boots as he went. He held the long water gun by its barrel, aiming it down at the top of his head, and with the insertion of a quarter engaged the works, disappearing into a vaporous high-pressure cone of suds and steam.

The rest of us stood about somewhat ill at ease. The oiler shortly had the presence of mind to offer Pampa and Borger a beer, and we adjusted into as comfortable a group as we could standing around a log truck drinking beer in a shut-down convenience-store parking lot watching Mr. Irony shower in a car wash. I personally felt negligible, and had for some time, and thought to remove myself from the affair, at least as a *dramatis persona*, it being arguable whether I was contributing much toward my narrative end of the stick; further arguable whether I would ever be able to demonstrate in telling fashion that I had in fact picked up self-deprecating ironic ways from Mr. Irony, whose student I allegedly was, and who (Mr. Irony) was, having finished his shower, walking sopping wet into Bill's Dollar Store next to the car wash. I could serve the tale best, I thought, and finally not without considerable self-deprecation and irony, by removing myself from it, and decided thereupon to do so, and hereby pronounce myself expunged from this affair as teller—

Pampa I intend to continue to have relations with, but that coupling is a private matter and is not to be hereafter mentioned. In point of fact, I had felt for two hundred butt-pounding rough miles that the oiler was the proper student of Mr. Irony, a figure of such unironic beginnings that something like true biblical salvation and conversion, if not a bona fide saintly transformation, was available to him if Mr. Irony attempted to bless him with the vision which would let him stop seeing as important his dead father-in-law and his life as minister of lubricant. Mr. Irony emerged from Bill's Dollar Store bearing gifts for the crew and for the Available Traveling Women and none for me—confirming me in my resolve to defect. A fair fare-thee-well to you all.

The presentation of gifts began with a stir—Mr. Irony presented Pampa and Borger with panty hose—"Apologies, ladies: not designer pants"—and persuaded them to don them in the cab of the log truck. When the women emerged, glossy-legged and matted, the crew and the insurance salesman all adopted a deliberately calmed-down demeanor like that of men in a bar before the storm of a bar fight.

Mr. Irony presented the driver with a case of Skoal, a particolored welder's cap made of dungaree cloth, and a Buck knife, which, as the driver reached for it, Mr. Irony threw into the adjacent wooded lot. "The knife is guaranteed for life, even against loss, sir." The driver donned his new cap, backwards, took a big pinch of Skoal, pocketed the fresh tin of snuff on his butt, looked sidelong at the panty-hosed women, and walked jauntily and juicy-lipped into the woods.

"A good man," Mr. Irony remarked. He pulled from

a carton a model 44 Husqvarna chain saw, started it, cut the air after the fashion of a Shriner with a big sequined sword, and motioned to the oiler to come relieve him of the saw.

"I don't cut," the oiler shouted over the saw.

"You cut," Mr. Irony bellowed back. "Cut that billboard down." Mr. Irony allowed the saw to idle.

"Taint gone fuck hisself *all* up," Rooster said.

"Mr. Rooster," Mr. Irony said, "shut the fuck up. Taint *ain't.*"

The oiler, carrying the saw somewhat apprehensively, at arm's length, addressed the billboard on which a candidate for sheriff promised to restore law and order to Dillon County, and cut through the first creosote pole with a clean, flexed, low turn of his body, one with the saw, and stepped to the next pole in the same crouch, and to the next and the next, and the candidate for sheriff fell on his face into the parking lot, blowing full beers off the log truck and crushing the insurance salesman's Blazer.

"Oh shit," the salesman said. The parking lot began to smell of perfume. "Oh God."

"Oh boy," Borger said.

"Yes, ma'am," Pampa said.

"No event is unplanned for the intelligent purveyor of insurance, is it, sir?" Mr. Irony said to the insurance salesman.

"What?"

"The readiness, I believe, is all, sir?"

"Not—not *cars*. I sell life insurance."

"Receive your gratuity, sir." Mr. Irony handed the salesman a boxed leisure suit the color of green mint dinner candies and a gun-style hair dryer. The suit had contrasting yellow stitching and the blower a barrel the size and shape of a grenade mortar, the opening of which the salesman was measuring with his spread hand. "Damn! I can *get* another car!" he suddenly said. "No problem! Hey!" He passed his fist into the hair dryer.

The oiler dropped the chain saw on the truck bed and opened two beers, taking a sip from each. He sat on the truck bed beside the saw and crossed his legs with an odd, pensive, pursed-lip expression on his face. Mr. Irony addressed him.

"You *do* cut, sir, and with élan."

"My knee start to give out on me."

"Understandable. You were configured as low and sturdy as Johnny Bench."

"*Down* there, wudden I?"

"Yessir."

"Got to fish sometime, right?"

"Right on."

"Can't cut bait all your life."

"No sir."

"Can't cut bait all your life, right?"

"You are right."

"Taint gone mess *up*," Rooster said.

"I ain't *tee*ther," Taint said.

"Mr. Rooster," Mr. Irony said, "Mr. Taint is in a rehabilitative power drive that needs no gainsaying."

"That his saw?"

" 'Tis."

"Gone give me them boots, homeboy?"

"Gone give you a boom box, mother."

From Bill's Dollar Store, a credenza-style home entertainment center is wheeled out on a four-wheel furniture dolly by two men who struggle over curbing to keep the dolly under it.

"That thing is seven foot *long*," Rooster said.

"Big enough for a boog like you," Taint said.

"You put that affair on your shoulder and it is yours. I have had it converted to 12 volts. Batteries included."

"Batteries?"

"Two Die Hards in the TV compartment, wired in parallel."

"You *trazee*."

"Hoist it up, Mr. Rooster."

"This some kind of *race* joke."

"Might be."

"Hey, Rooster. So what?" the oiler said to Rooster. "*So fucking what?*"

"You done mess that boy *up*," Rooster said to Mr. Irony.

Mr. Irony and the two Bill's Dollar employees and the oiler got under one end of the home entertainment center and, like the Marines on the flagpole at Iwo Jima, shouldered it up to a 60-degree angle. The oiler waved impatiently at Rooster to get under the giant radio.

Rooster obliged, shaking his head, and lifted the machine without noticeable strain. He took a step backwards, kicking the dolly free, and hefted the home entertainment center an inch or two forwards and backwards for balance. He swung it, like a sail boom, through an arc, looking for the others.

"I'll say this to his *face*," the oiler said to Mr. Irony. "You are one buck nigger, Rooster."

"You right, Daddydied. Turn this thing *on*."

From the truck bed, the oiler leaned over and reached inside the long box, and suddenly the lot was overwhelmed with a booming radio broadcast. Rooster started to jive. He got clear of the truck, clear of the billboard, everyone backed off to give him room, and he began a blaster walk, a walk of total indifference to the world, a series of steps and half steps and backsteps, around the parking lot of the closed convenience store in Dillon, S.C.

He circled back by the group, now holding its ears. "Don't want your boots now, homeboy. This all right," he shouted. To the oiler: "Okay, Taint. Don't call me a nigger ever again. You earn that first one."

"Ladies," he said, bowing slightly to the Available Traveling Women, the entertainment center tipping as slowly and heavily as a ship on a swell. "I'm going to go see some of the brothers." He left the lot in the gliding, halting, butt-clenching locomotion required of a proper dude beneath a seven-foot-long, 200-pound, 80-watt-per-channel, fake-walnut-veneer, credenza-style home entertainment center.

Grease and oil—and that's not all, I do hydraulic and seals and packing leathers—grease and oil is very important. It is not just, as far as a lubricant. I believe it is like the blood of machines. Not the energy—that's your gas—but the blood, as far as life. Machine life. Saw life. Splitter life. Truck life. Backhoe life. And tools make men's life easier. Oil is the blood of the dirt. We buried Lumpy's Daddy Saddy. I'm okay now.

I was not for a spot there. Then we carried a fellow on the log boom thew might all Georgia that said shape up and Rooster fucked with me and I just, I don't know, got right over it. He was, special to me, as far as almost being my own father, I thought sometimes.

My real daddy a preacher. But Lumpy daddy, before we even got married, one day he explained to me what viscosity means. That is a word I deal with. One day he give me a beer and a bowl of hot chili and he say, That— pointing to the beer—is not viscosity, and that—pointing to the chili—is viscosity. That might sound obvious to me now, but it was not obvious to me then. It was a hot chili, too. Lumpy daddy make a good chili.

I'm okay now.

Mr. Irony came to see me later that afternoon in Pampa's and my suite—Pepe's El Presidente Suite at South of the Border, where *Duke* recommends Men at Their Best recuperate from log-truck carriage—came to me and asked that I not make myself so scarce, explaining that "things" need me. I asked him what that was intended to mean. He said again: "Well, things need you, son."

I pondered this a moment, and it occurred to me that he somehow knew of my decision to remove myself from this account of our world tour—I had not informed him of that decision; nor, for that matter, was he, I thought at the time, aware that there *was* an account. A character in a sombrero and serape jingled on spurs into the room where we sat and announced, "The senōritas expect youse for margaritas at the Acapulco Pulquería Número Three-a." We said okay. Mr. Irony handed him a fifty-dollar bill and he left with a flourish of his serape and a jingle of spurs.

"I was at risk as your student, I thought. The oiler guy looked like he was better raw material."

"Pshaw. Never edge him up right. Buck him up, yes. Stop that damned whimpering, yes. But the proper attitude of self-unimportance would cast him back into the aquarium in which he died. He did resemble, as you noted, the decaying Plectostomus you found as a child that shocked you because you thought it, for weeks, merely *not moving.*"

"Sir, you know everything I think?"

"Stop just short of everything."

"What don't you know, then? You said you stop short of—"

"You have had, I believe you confessed, my Traveling Woman while we've been Men at Our Best?"

"Yes."

"Well. There are certain *final things*, in the nature of excretions and animal noises and the quality of ardor, that I choose not to know."

"I see. But you *could.*"

"I could."

"Because you are—is omniscient a meaningful term?"

"Left field. Nothing of the kind. *Happy hour!*"

With that, Mr. Irony left the suite, headed for the Acapulco Pulquería Número Three-a.

Mr. Irony Renounces Irony

$\mathbf{I}$ **M**r. Irony renounced irony and took his place in line at Unemployment. Where once he would have found the tedium of the protracted process a delight, akin to the moves of a child's board game, he found the desk-to-desk ordeal—and getting in the wrong line, and then getting in the right line to have it closed when he was one party from the bureaucrat serving it—officious, small-minded, forgiveless horseshit.

With a sheaf of papers so bulky that he longed for a briefcase to hold them in, he stood on one pained leg or the other lamenting his decision to quit irony. It left him uninsulated against the world, as if he had renounced drink or drugs instead. Despair came after him—with little tentacles it reached toward his balding head from the low fiberboard ceiling tiles of the Unemployment Office complex. "I rue the day I quit irony," he remarked to the woman behind him.

"I wish I hadn't quit Toys "Я" Us," the woman said.

Despite himself, Mr. Irony felt a small thrill at her response. It was, with his remark . . . no, he was through with irony. Fourteen hours later, on their third shift of unemployment counselors, the same woman spoke to him again: "Honey, you didn't really *quit* your job, did you?"

At this instant Mr. Irony conceived of his Desired Vocation, still a blank line on several of his multitudinous forms. He wanted to be a circus rider, a trick rider of horses going in a circle, standing on them, flipping backwards on them, maybe flipping backwards from one to the other . . .

"I'm worrit about you, mister," the woman was saying. "I don't think you know *the ropes.*"

"Why not?"

"The way you *stan* there. You can' stan there that way, all tired like, if you ever done this before. We ain't begin to get *no*where. I'm fraid you *did* quit your job."

"Of *course* I quit my job," Mr. Irony said, worried that the woman had somehow detected his enjoyment in the irony of her quitting Toys "Я" Us and his quitting irony.

"Child," she said, "you can' *quit*. You got to be *fire*. You *quit*, but you git them to *fire* your ass. You quit in your *heart*, but you git fire *on paper.*"

"Maybe I was fired," Mr. Irony said.

"If you was, you *know.*"

"Actually, I never really had a *job*, I had a—"

"Honey, none us ever had no *job*. Who want *that?*"

"I had a . . . style, you might say."

The woman looked at him with a grin. "You was

some kind *pimp*, I bet. I like them miscegenational pimps—"

"No, madam, it's—"

"Hell. Don' get snitty."

It was going to be a hard life, Mr. Irony saw. Without something to fill the void left by the departure of his vice, he was going to be subject to humorless days until he got high on something else. Christ was out of the question, precisely because He Himself contained no small measure of irony. Even getting high on "life itself" sounded inappropriately ironic. Only being a . . . circus rider made, at the moment, any kind of clean, unironical sense.

There would be no irony in standing on a horse, if you could. And if the horse moved in a circle, that was its business. And if you had to put on some tights and a sequined vest and some special slippers, and the horse had to wear some flashy, colorful hardware, that was show business. He did not see how a man who had renounced irony could go wrong being a circus rider.

He began trying to fill in Desired Vocation on his forms against his thigh. The woman behind him bent over also to see what he was writing.

"Circus rider. That's a good one," she said. "You catchin on. You *never* get hire."

Even though there was a rich incense of irony about this woman and everything she said, Mr. Irony liked her. He looked at her fondly and she got down on her hands and knees.

"This the best part of Unemployment, honey. Put them foams on my back and write all you wont to. It feels *good*. Don't poke *too* hard or you'll come through."

Mr. Irony did as he was told, and used the human desk as it and he moved incrementally toward their benefits.

Back at his apartment, Mr. Irony had a seizure, or something like a seizure. It was probably equivalent to the withdrawal anxiety common to boozers or druggers, only his fear was uncharted: he was sailing for the first time in the troubled, mundane waters of life without irony. It made him stand glumly beside the refrigerator, knowing that opening it and bending and looking at all the things—cruddy-lipped mustard jars, two olives in a tall bottle, a Baggie full of rotten parsley, a small German roach moving very slowly—that used to delight him in their queer combinations was not a pleasure open to him now. As a young man he had lost his women and lost his mind; as an older man he had lost money and his mind; now he had lost his irony, and it had never been this bad. Women and money were nothing to irony.

At the Unemployment Office he had been denied benefits because he had had no employer. His case worker finally did not doubt that he might have been fired after reading his aptitude questionnaire (under skills, Mr. Irony listed "left-handed"). When the issue of self-employment was broached, Mr. Irony denied stringently that he had been his own employer, a flatly ironic notion and one therefore not available to a reformed ironic. The entire affair—two days and six hours and forty-eight minutes from taking a number to being dismissed as ineligible for benefits—which once would have made his day, or week, was as disappointing as it would have been to the common fools down there trying to get something for nothing. He realized, finally, standing by the refrigerator, just before he opened it and *ate* the two olives and *scared* the roach and *squeezed* a green juice from the parsley Baggie, that *being down there* had been off limits; what was more ironic than getting paid for not working *only* if you could prove someone had deemed you *unsuitable* for working? Why couldn't you be paid for not working if you were suitable? Only the unfit benefit. It was not Darwinian. It was ironic. It had been, he saw now, a close call, close to a "slip" in the parlance of reforming abusers of substance and, he supposed it was fair to regard himself, abusers of style. He was a reforming abuser of style, a reforming ironic.

There were no books for him, no post- or pre-traumatic stress syndromes, no Adult Children of Ironic Parents groups to go to, no women counselors that spent their lives holding your hand if you'd had too much fun abusing something and now wanted as recompense to hold hands with idle women. No nothing. He was alone. He might have been on Mars. This gave him comfort. At least he was not in a herd of whiners who pulled out a poker chip and explained its significance before they told you their name. Mr. Irony resolved he would carry a cow chip before a poker chip, if that was not ironic— already, he was relieved to discover, he was not sure what irony was. A positive sign.

Still, he was pretty certain that extracting from the pocket in a somber, proud, ceremonious fashion and confidentially beginning to explain to an innocent by-stander that what this cow chip represented was . . . was ironic. Perhaps he could, for a while, find a substitute for irony. Substitute therapy was common, even if it itself was perhaps a little ironic.

He had recently witnessed a father and young daughter purchasing some candy for the mother's birthday. The child, who was allowed to select the candy, decided on chocolate-covered peanuts, and decided that they were "pretend poops." Indeed, the candies had looked like small, hard turds.

"But don't *tell* Mommy we're giving her pretend poops," the father instructed.

The child grinned wickedly. "It'll be . . . *pretty surprisy!*"

That, Mr. Irony thought, might be an acceptable substitute for *ironic*: *surprisy*. Irony he could quit, but, as methadone to his heroin, he could not quit that which was surprisy.

"Surprisy it is, then," he announced, still leaning against the refrigerator, immediately looking less glum. He then crawled out of his own kitchen window and crawled back in. It felt good. He felt fine. Not himself, but all right.

"All surprising *right*," he said, beginning a rubber-legged dance that came to him. He bandied this way through the apartment, saying "Surprise *you!*" to walls and paintings and furnishings. He told everything to surprise off. "Just get the surprise out of my way," he said to a pair of boxer shorts, and deftly toed them—through an incredibly long arc—into the clothes hamper. Suddenly, badly, he wanted a uniformed maid working full time in his small apartment, altogether too small for such a servant, and he wanted *only new clothes*.

Piling all of his old clothes into a heap, and thinking of how he might safely present himself at the haberdasher's *naked*, he paused to congratulate himself: not just any man could kick irony once it had its teeth in him. A lesser man, one less surprisy, would have failed.

The Modern Italian

    I   **M**ario Moscalini passed on his way out the door every morning one of several Michelin guides to Italy that were kept open to his favorite passage about modern Italy. He sometimes glanced at the books, but he had long before memorized the passage:

Modern Italy.—In this land abounding in every type of beauty, the modern Italian lives and moves with perfect ease. Dark-haired, black-eyed, gesticulating, nimble and passionate, he is all movement and fantasy.

This overflowing vitality appears in many modern achievements that may surprise the visitor. Improvement of the soil, industrial complexes, nuclear power centres, dams, motorways and skyscrapers, characterize the fantastic economic development which has taken place after World War II, giving Italy a new look and belying the legend of the macaroni-eating, guitar-playing Italian. A new way of life has been created in the country.

On Mario, one such modern Italian, these words had the calming, assuring effect of a psalm.

He was thinking specifically of the moving about modern Italy with perfect ease as he whipped his taxi through the customs gates at the port of Livorno to pick up his first fare of the day, a merchant seaman. Mario liked sailors. Unlike regular tourists, they were not finicky about what they wanted to see or do or where they wanted to go. They wanted food, women, to sleep, and they spoke in a direct fashion. With a sailor Mario was free to be himself, a man.

The sailor this morning was well-fed-looking, and Mario was not surprised to hear him ask for a *"puta"* right away. He turned to the sailor and said, with a conspiratorial wink, "I have large size."

"Not a fat one," the sailor said.

"No," Mario said, "you do not seize my meaning. *I* have large size." He held up his arm, flexed, his fist touching the ceiling of the cab.

"Non capisco Italiano," the sailor said.

"You not must to know Italiano. In plain English, I have large size." He winked again.

"Let me out," the sailor said.

"But we are not to *la puntana* so *presto—*"

"You take her," the sailor said, stepping from the moving taxi and running down the street.

Mario Moscalini was nimble enough, to be sure, to have caught the man, but it was just a matter of a language barrier, or something, and the skipped fare was not large, so he elected to just move on with traffic. Later he regretted this decision somewhat, because the day proved very dull, and it would have been enlivening to

have stopped the sailor and wildly demanded his fare—
and more, as reparation for the rudeness—and generally
to have demonstrated to the fool what passion can mean.
The man had been at sea too long for his own good.

It was not until he was on his way home that things
picked up. He was tired, and it was funny the way it
worked, but the best things seemed to happen to him
when he was too tired to avail himself of golden opportunity. And if ever a golden opportunity bore down on
him, it did as he clicked off his duty lights. He saw
Cicciolina, pornostar and parliamentarian, by the side of
the road, alone and needing a ride. She was supposed to
be in Rome making legislation or movies. But she was
here under a streetlight. Something was wrong, entirely
out of place, so he got her into the cab without pressing
her for an explanation. She would volunteer her troubles
if she wanted to. Mario respected a person's privacy if
he respected anything in the world. And he respected
l'onorevole Cicciolina if he respected any*one* in the world.
If she had not had the sense to pull her dress up over
her *tette* at her press conference at Piazza Navona in
Rome when she won her seat in parliament, he had been
told that the very irreplaceable Bernini fountain there
could have been much more seriously damaged than it
was. People acted as if they had never seen *tette* before.
It was ridiculous. Still, hers were a bit special, they looked
good in movies, and it made him wonder if they were
like movie stars themselves—maybe not so great-looking
in real life. He thought she would be glad to show them
to him, even if she was in some kind of trouble, so he
turned down an oddly unfamiliar street—he knew Livorno backwards, he thought—where he could park if

she agreed to a showing, and they were suddenly surrounded by the blue lights of *polizia*. How could she be in trouble with the law? She *was* the law.

An officer approached Mario's window, pointing adamantly in the direction they had come. Then he threw his arms to heaven and shook his head. Mario saw now the one-way signs he had—it was incredible—been going against. And he a professional driver. That was why the officer was so wild in his gesticulations probably. Mario had let down the fraternity of professional men on the road. He got out to face the officer.

When the officer again pointed and raised his arms in total surrender at a move so *un*nimble as Mario's, Mario fell to his knees and sculpted giant breasts in the air before his chest as he had seen Greek sailors do many times when they danced in the port bars.

He was overcome by a passion that had not seized him so in the car—he suddenly knew why men had broken a foot off a river god when they saw *l'onorevole* Cicciolina's *tette*. "Her *tette* were *credimi, eccellente— grande, pesante—*"

"Whose?" the officer said.

"*L'onorevole* Cicciolina's."

"When?"

"Now."

"Now?"

"She was in the taxi with me—it's why I took the bad turn—"

"Where is she now?"

"Disappeared, apparently. You did not see her?"

"No."

"She's fast. It's almost incredible, but I think she's

in trouble with the law. That's why she vamooshed. Is she wanted by the law?"

"You were in a fantasy," the officer said.

"I doubt it." Mario met the officer eye to eye. He held his ground. "I doubt that extremely."

The officer pursed his lips. "Good for you. No ticket today. *Buon viaggio.* I'd like to meet her, too. Here's my number."

"*Ciao*," Mario said. He doubted that *l'onorevole* Cicciolina would consort with *polizia* but he held his tongue. Let the officer dream.

He sped homeward, thinking that if the officer had not been one policeman but a whole band of carabinieri with Uzis, and they had opened fire, he and Cicciolina would have looked a lot like Warren Beatty and Faye Dunaway in *Bonnie and Clyde,* except his Fiat was a little smaller than Clyde's coupe, and Cicciolina's *tette* were a lot larger than Bonnie Parker's. He threw the officer's number out the window, an act he would regret when he got home.

At his house the first thing he saw was a man looking into his windows. Fearing he might be an assassin, perhaps some new form of competition among taxi drivers, he circled the block until the man disappeared, discovering in his revolutions that his Fiat, though now getting on in miles, still got good rubber going into both second and third. When the man had gone, he realized that a taxi-driver assassin would not linger in the *absence* of a taxi, so he was probably fantasizing a bit, but still, you could not rule anything out these days. You have CIA, the Israelis are back-to-the-wall, look at Libya, and the French can be so snotty. Mario had had nightmares since hearing in childhood about tiny Frenchmen with wires who had been deadly on Germans who were caught patrolling lines—from behind, total surprise, wire through neck. There was an air of lunacy about it, but Mario thought it just could have been a lost Frenchman looking to kill him for some fantastic reason, kill him with a wire, if it was still true that they were good with the wire.

Getting out of his car, Mario stepped on a wire. This nearly gave him an *infarto*. But he saw, before he stopped breathing altogether, that it was only his radio antenna that he had yanked two mornings ago from the red hands of the neighbor's six-year-old. He had given the child a very stern talking-to about antenna stealing leading straight to bank robbing and jail, gesticulating with a razor motion at his throat. The child, still holding the snapped-off antenna, did not seem to understand, so Mario choked himself until blue to demonstrate the effects of hanging as he had seen them in Westerns. At this the child dropped the antenna and ran off laughing. Mario left it there. It was not sightly to reconnect a ripped-out antenna, and less sightly to stick in its place a coat hanger. Besides, his radio did not work. It had blown out one night as he passed a nuclear power station. He had a vaguely dishonest feeling after scolding the child, because the radio was useless and because he had himself wanted to be a bank robber before circumstances led him into taxi driving.

He approached his house with caution. Seeing no one, he entered. The house was wide open and well lit. It looked to have been robbed. Drawers and closets were open, some of his wife's dresses were on the bed, others hanging askew on their hangers half out of the closet. He checked immediately beneath his pillow for his pistol, a German officer's Luger which he had purchased from a man at a flea market who had restored the finish expertly and filled the barrel with lead. His gun was there. So, for a heist, they had not been cleaned out. The scum had missed the real treasure.

In the kitchen he expected to find the pasta water on and, by extension, his wife, but she was not there. There was a note on the kitchen table. He looked under the kitchen sink to see if the bastards had found his shoeshine kit. They had not. It was safe. The little kiwi birds on the brush handles looked at him serenely, as if to say, *We held our ground.*

He wanted to get the pasta going but couldn't decide on what type. He stopped just before salting the water, sat down at the table absently eating rock salt, and looked at the note. It was, apparently, from his wife. The salt was very salty, he noticed. He decided to secure the doors and windows against a return of the scavengers and sit in the dark waiting for them. He had seen the American detective Mannix and perhaps Jack Nicholson in *China-town* do this. They couldn't tell where you were, but you could see them by the streetlights outside. What was dangerous in this case was that they would not be able to see his Luger. If he lit a candle, perhaps they could see the gun, and maybe just enough of him, like Marlon Brando in *Apocalypse Now,* that he would look terribly menacing and slender. Also, he could read his wife's note. It was beginning to interest him.

By the light of the candle, his wife's note, weighted down attractively by his Luger diagonally across it, was a pretty thing. It was note-sized, a handsome cut stationery, not a hastily torn-off scrap of something larger. His wife's hand was neat, clear, strong for a woman. She had written, apparently, if this was her writing—he thought it was—that she was leaving, that she had found another man, and that he, Mario, didn't know beans about large size. Mario shook his head: it was just like her. She was always carrying on about large size. *She* was the one who didn't know beans about large size. A boyhood friend of his had been called Hannibal in Gymnasium, "because he comes over the mountain with an elephant between his legs." But Mario had been called Scipio, "who surrounded Hannibal." That was large size. "She not to know no bean about no large size," Mario said aloud in the dark, pointing the Luger at the neat note. "She needs a hole small-size in her brainpan small-size."

His English was at its best, he felt, when he was stressed by something, and he liked to exercise it in non-conversational modes like this. The feeling it gave him was that of writing poetry. With English, he might have been Petrarch. He had heard that a very similar liberation had visited the writer Joseph Conrad.

He ate some more salt and thought further of the assassin. Was he this alleged lover? The carrier of large size? He was not the burglar. The burglar would not have been looking in at the mess he had himself made, unless he was looking to see if he had missed something. But what could you tell you had missed from outside when you had missed it *inside*? That was fantasy. What if the man had not been a taxi assassin or a thief but a voyeur, looking to get a peek at him and his wife having their frequent relationships?

This was of paramount concern to Mario. The sanctity of their marriage would have been sullied by interloper's eyes. Holy images would have been boot-legged by a common criminal into the street, perhaps for the amusement of the pervert's colleagues in scum. He could see a gang of purse thieves in Naples sitting around about three hundred purses talking about his large size and his delirious wife. The delicate sculpture of their fond embrace—joined as artfully as marble, her legs per-haps thrashing over his clenched back—would be dis-located from its hallowed pediment and carried like spoils into the mean secular minds of the equivalent of ma-rauding Gauls. They were the same people who whapped the genitals and noses off all the sculpture of Italy. He had seen sculpted *infants* mutilated by these people who had looked into his house.

Mario pulled the drapes and went to bed. It was dangerous to let his imagination go. Besides, he had an early fare, a Frenchman with a travel-guide company who wanted to see Livorno, all of it. It was a flat day rate.

He went to sleep wondering if there was a subtle way of frisking a man for a wire. He could simply say, *Regolazione nuova!* and feel him up. There were two problems with this. One, the Frenchman might be—he had heard so many were—homosexual. A man such as Mario could never be too careful in this regard. Two, a wire is hard to feel, certainly nothing like his Luger, an honest weapon. He might miss the wire, relax, even get comfortable with the garrote expert, and, while talking about, say, Jerry Lewis movies with the killer . . . a knobby, hot chain through his esophagus with two little jerks, *left*, *right*—no, he put it all from his mind. He could not afford to let his imagination do irrational things. He needed his sleep. It was a good thing, really, his wife was not present to pester him all night. He would be in no shape to defend himself.

When he picked up his Frenchman the next morning, he marveled at the accuracy of *rana*, the pejorative applied to the French, he had always thought, with no basis except in fantasy. Now he saw, instead, that *frog* was no fantasy, no pejorative even. The man attempting to wedge himself into the cab was jowled, top-heavy, and looking at him through eyeglasses that so magnified his eyes—in fact, his whole upper face—that Mario, looking into the man's pupils, which were the size of roasted chestnuts, thought he saw things in them. It was crazy, but he thought he saw a yo-yo in the frog's left eye. It was something round and moving around on a string, that much was for sure.

The Frenchman packed himself in finally and pushed his heavy, green-tinted glasses up onto his nose, which adjustment made his eyes even larger. It was like looking into windows at an aquarium. Mario saw, deep in the black pools, what he thought were the two little white sphincters of the optic nerve junctions.

"What are you looking at?" the Frenchman asked.

"Can you see me, masseur?"

"Too well," the Frenchman said.

Mario was relieved to hear the Frenchman could see. Taking a tourist, much less a travel writer, who could not see around all day to see things was not his idea of fun. "Masseur, excuse me if I appear unkept. I was up most night without sleep."

"I see. Your manners are ruined by restlessness. You are all movement even at night."

The words *all movement* startled Mario. He did not know why.

The Frenchman whipped out a small notebook and wrote something down. On the cover of the notebook Mario saw a small inflated doughy figure of a man he recognized—the tiny, bulbous Michelin man. *All movement! All movement and fantasy!* From the psalm of the modern Italian in modern Italy who belied the legends. It was fantastic! The man might have even been the writer of the Scripture! Mario intended to ask but was now absorbed by how much the Frenchman resembled not only a frog but the Michelin logo itself, the pneumatic, happy clown that sold tires for the largest tire manufacturer in the world. How had Michelin gotten a writer who just so evoked the company image? Had they based the logo on this man? Had they other men in the employ who looked like the clown? The possibilities were many. It was all fantastic. Suddenly he could see beneath the soft, froggy exterior only his concern of the night before— a piano wire cinched into the corpulence with the apparent innocence of just another ring of fat, of which there might be hundreds. It would be useless to frisk the Frenchman—he would never even detect a gun in all that meat.

"Masseur, I have dread to give offense, because so *presto* I seize that you may be a much important writer personally to me. But if you are making to carry a wire, it will be *vietato*."

As soon as he delivered himself of this warning, he felt foolish. The Frenchman was so tightly packed into the cab that his arms were pinned immobile against the doors. Only in fantasy was there danger. "Anyway," he said, by way of apology, "one wire would not hurt much."

The Frenchman glared at him.

At the first bar they passed, a favorite of his, Mario jumped out and went in and got himself a *caffè*, leaving the Frenchman stuffed in the standing cab. He told Neutro, the bartender, that he was tempted to multiply the day rate by three because he had three times the weight of one man in his taxi. "Such a thing would be perfectly legal," he said.

"Such a thing would anger. You are not capable of so fantastic a suggestion."

"Such a thing must to have a opposite and a equal reaction, Neutro. Newton, Sir Isaac."

Neutro shrugged. Mario was forever quoting science to him. They were equals as nonpracticing scientists.

Mario drank a tall glass of mineral water and announced, "Neutro, I once saw a flea drink a glass of water and swell to twice its original size."

"Preposterous. You know full well, *Dottore*, that the flea would burst. Bernouli."

"You contradict me?"

"Science herself contradicts you, Mario Moscalini."

"A cognac *portare via*."

"As you will."

Outside, Mario carefully handed in the pony of cognac to the Frenchman, who struggled to get his hands up to take the glass, but appeared to be genuinely grateful. Mario cautioned himself that this might be entirely his imagination. He could not trust a man this large, this unpassionate, this unnimble.

Getting in the cab, Mario saw, across the street, carrying a large loaf of bread and waving cheerfully at him, his wife. This was curious, because there was no bakery nearby. He decided at that moment to drive the Frenchman first to the large new vineyards of his friends the Buffala brothers, because he knew that the Michelin guide did not yet contain reference to a business so new. And if the Frenchman's appetite for the morning cognac was any sign—he had poured it smoothly into his mouth in one motion of his tiny, cramped hands and sighed appreciatively, almost whimpered—there was a good bet he might have a good time tasting the Buffalas' special wines.

Passing the spot where the sailor had jumped fare on him the day before, Mario again saw his wife. How she got across town so fast was a mystery. She waved to him again but, he thought, not quite so cheerfully this time. She will see, he thought. She will learn. He looped the block several times looking for the sailor. It was fantasy, of course, to expect to find him, but he was prepared to be illogical if that was the only price for avenging yesterday's loss. He stopped at a second bar for a second *caffè* and another cognac for the wedged Frenchman. He phoned the Buffala brothers to warn them he was bringing so important a tourist.

"Adriano, for this one, I suggest you say the wine is radioactive. That is best with a Frenchman. They are advanced."

"The radioactive defense, you think?"

"Yes. You do not want a Frenchman considering mummies. They don't believe in that. They are advanced."

"Well, why not tell him the truth?"

"Oofah, Adriano. You are fantastic. He wants to believe in the modern Italy, and he is health-conscious.

He has a lot to be conscious of, too. He is big. Tap a keg, my advice to you."

"All right. I will find Germano and get our story straight."

On the way, Mario told the Frenchman that there was an ugly rumor concerning the strange potency and unique flavor of the Buffala brothers' new wine. "They have had *un sacco di* success with this wine, my friend. It is a product verily of the modern Italy. But of course, with success, with a sack of success, you have a sack of talk."

"How far is it?" the Frenchman asked. "If it is far, stop for another aperitif, I'll remain aboard." It was like a clever Frenchman to feign uninterest in the slander of successful wine.

"It has been said that the heavy bocket and the risputed hallucinogenic quality—a California wholesaler is very interesting in this—is because the soil is refused from a nuclear power station fuel dump and the grapes, they have changed mutationally in one generation or less to a new fruit. Mendel, Gregor."

This was all baloney. The nuclear defense which Mario was setting up was just a herring to keep people from thinking certain other theories regarding the weird wine. These theories were all supplied by the Buffala brothers. It was policy to tender the theory they wanted a given customer to swallow, and then to deny it less vigorously than they denied the competing theories, which they discreetly let slip out. Once a customer was sottoed on the wine, and the psychology correctly applied, he believed the wine special for reasons he found comforting, or credible, and bought, as it were, *sacks* of it. "That is how you have a sack of success," the Buffala brothers were fond of saying. "You *sell* sacks of it."

What was special about the wine actually varied from week to week. Benzine was getting too expensive, isopropyl was boring. This week they were using ethylene glycol—antifreeze. The third Buffala brother, Sevriano, was a psychiatrist, and he was the technical adviser to his brothers, the true vintners. He was also the originator of all the rumors and the psychology of their applications, and he was the only one among the brothers who did not at least partially subscribe to one or several of the bogus stories at any given moment. Sevriano had taken his training in Paris. Germano and Adriano put the contaminants in the wine themselves, yet they found themselves arguing the logic, and finally the truth, of the fictions, or marketing strategies, as Sevriano liked to call them. What was special about the wine had been summed up neatly once by a redheaded American hippie, who commented after his first two bottles, "Man, this is some bad shit," and bought all he could carry on his back.

Mario Moscalini also had trouble maintaining a purchase on what was really the matter with the wine, but he had proved remarkably adept at adducing the psychologies of prospective buyers and getting them to subscribe to a working marketing strategy. He had been so adept that Sevriano had considered making him a Buffala brother, which was not a difficult thing to do, since the Buffala brothers were not brothers.

To the Frenchman, whose eye was peeled for a bar and another cognac, Mario now delivered the denial phase of the nuclear-mutation strategy. "This mutation calendar is a clear false," he said. "They found some welding rods on the site. That is all." The denial was so weak it convicted of the contrary—Mario thought it was like saying, *I didn't kill him, I just shot him a little.*

The Frenchman produced his notebook and made a note in it. "Calumny," he said, and chuckled. He might chuckle, Mario thought, but it will work. He is a nuclear man if I ever saw one. The French are advanced. After about two bottles of the wine, he would look at the bottle, and then at the ground, and then at his hand that had touched the bottle. The question would then not be far off: "How'd this nuclear waste thing get going, Signor Buffala?" And Adriano and Germano would laugh and deny it all, and the Frenchman would feel so buzzedly *good* sitting there as they brought him another bottle that he would actually *like* the idea of a mutant wine, a wine with even a little radioactivity itself in it—that's how they treat cancer, with a little fire, you fight fire with fire and this fire feels *good*.

Today Mario did like the nuclear business, perhaps because he was yet mindful of his radio having blown out driving by a power station. The other defenses were also attractive at times. Some rather romantic, if not downright somber, types went for a strategy that posited Etruscan, or earlier, tombs beneath the vines, and featured the hungry tips of the grapevine roots tubering into ancient skulls, even into still oily bandages that covered 2,500-year-old human organs resembling carrots and peas. An accident in which a tractor had slipped out of gear had resulted in the tractor pulling up a large vine with a whole mummy wrapped in the roots. A giant, subterranean den of vipers could be advanced if the client appeared remotely Satanic, though they had never worked out a responsible scenario for how the poisons might get into the vines—it was preposterous that sensible snakes would bite plants. Oversexed folk, or for that matter those that might be judged undersexed, fell prey to an account of a buried cache of aphrodisiacs sent north by Cleopatra during troubles at Carthage. These strategies could be pitted against one another in endless shadings of credibility and incredibility, and it really didn't seem to matter how they were blended or denied if you could get one honestly laced bottle down the hatch.

They had no trouble getting a bottle down the hatch of the advanced Frenchman. During the first two—the customary complimentary dosage used to ply a prospective buyer—the Frenchman disported himself about as any other corpulent, half-drunk foreigner. On schedule, he did at one point look at his bottle, then at the ground, and then at the hand that had held the bottle. Most customers here began to compose reasons for being on their way with wine for the road. But the Frenchman drained his current bottle by turning it to the sky, then sighted through the green bottom of it into the heavens and asked that another bottle be opened. "I'm treating myself for cancer," he announced, a remark that struck Mario and the Buffala brothers as on the nail. Mario could diagnose—he had a fantastic nose for diagnostic marketing.

Mario and the Buffala brothers continued to nimbly and passionately accommodate the Frenchman. There was of course no calculating the benefit to accrue from a mention in the Michelin guide. Mario was just a little disconcerted at the length of time the Frenchman wanted to drink. This was predictable enough; it was not uncommon for the large man who would think nuclear to want to dawdle. But Mario had seen, while entertaining the Frenchman with some gesticulations about the absurdity of mummies, his wife pass between rows of grapevines several hundred yards from where they sat.

What was decidedly puzzling about this was that she appeared positively cheerful again. He had clocked her as losing that rosy aspect by now. If she was still cheerful in this absurd dalliance, he wanted immediately to go home and secure the house against her inevitable return. For surely that's where she would go when all this false cheer wore off, when she came out of her fantasy of wanting another man. Another thing that was fantastic was the amount of walking she was doing. This was not like her. She never walked anywhere. That is how Mario came to marry her. Every day for three months he found her in his cab. Every day she looked better and better in the rearview mirror. Mario knew the absurdity of that— no one could possibly look better *each day* for three months. Even if you started with some kind of warty witch, in three months of absolute improvement, you'd be somewhere beyond Helen of Troy, whom Mario regarded as the equivalent of the speed of light in women. You do not go beyond the speed of light, in physics or in women.

It was safer just to say that his wife grew on him. One day he looked up and said into the mirror, "If you married me you would save a lot of money. I would have to drive you around for nothing." So they got married, and Mario stopped raising the flag on his meter when she got in his cab. And he took her everywhere. In that respect, his proposition might have been imprudent. But otherwise their marriage had been happy, until this fantasy of hers. To see her walking was perhaps the hardest evidence yet that she had lost her senses. It made Mario extremely uncomfortable to be out in the Buffala vineyard working a large sale while subject, conceivably, to a sudden assault by, or confrontation with, his crazy wife. That was private business, to say the least.

"Your wife, signore," Mario suddenly heard, making him for a moment wild-eyed.

"Your wife," again. It was the Frenchman.

"My wife *what*, masseur?"

"Your wife—does she gesticulate passionately and is she all movement?" With this, curiously, the Frenchman stood unsteadily up and began to paw the ground with his dainty shoe.

So relieved was Mario that she had not been seen approaching them that he uncharacteristically revealed an intimate matter. "She has great desire and above normal accommodation. She has to. I have large size."

"I would like to meet her," the Frenchman slurred.

This remark had a most curious effect on Mario. It seemed to come from the mouth of the officer who had spoken of wanting to meet Cicciolina as well as from the mouth of the advanced Frenchman, and it seemed as if this rather hybrid speaker were somehow speaking of wanting to meet the same person. Yet the officer was not the Frenchman, and Cicciolina was not his wife. What a fantastic blend of lunacies that was. He and the Buffala brothers were supposed to be drinking good wine—he wondered if they had made an error and got some of the house stuff. All he could do, under the circumstances, was try to be as sane as possible. That was his advice to himself whenever things got strange: Be as sane as possible.

The sanest thing he could imagine was that the Frenchman must know something about his wife. The most practical way for that to be true would be if it had been the Frenchman she had run off with. It was a fact that the Frenchman *was* large-size. Whether he *had* large size was open to speculation. The sanest thing to do here would be to ask the Frenchman to take down his pants, but that might mess up the Michelin mention. The next sanest thing Mario could think of was that it had been the Frenchman prowling his house the night before, and that he might have seen his wife inside, before she took off on her fantasy. It could, in this light, be a quite innocent question from the advanced Frenchman, under the circumstances. Still, this left the fact that the Frenchman was at least a prowler. It had been dark and visibility poor, especially since Mario had not slowed down when he saw the figure at his windows, but he could have sworn that the man was smaller than the present Frenchman, that it had been one of the wiry variety allegedly good with the wire on the German lines in the war. He really didn't know what to think, and not knowing what to think—feeling things slip a little in his head—made Mario more nervous than the prospect of his deranged wife rushing up to them and making some kind of scene, possibly involving the relative sizes of himself and the giant, advanced, intoxicated, sweating Frenchman that they so badly wanted to make a favorable impression upon.

"I would like to meet your wife," the Frenchman said again, confirming Mario in his belief that there was a connection between his fare for the day and his perambulating wife, and firming his resolve to think as sanely as possible through the mess and act accordingly. He decided that the best thing to do would be to bury the Frenchman alive. Whether they put him in with the mummies, or fed him to the vipers, or burned him slowly to death with hot nuclear wastes, or exploded his giant desire with an overdose of Cleopatra's aphrodisiacs was of no concern to Mario—you could not predict what would *really* happen in the mind of a large, advanced Frenchman under a vineyard. They only had to dig a good, fat hole and put the fat frog in it and cover it up. He was suddenly very passionate about his lack of concern for the Frenchman's fantastic psychology.

"My wife is of no concern to me, masseur," Mario said. "I would call some of my large girlfriendship if I had not lost my address book in the burglary."

The Frenchman pursed his lips and gave Mario a squinty look he had seen somewhere before. For a moment he thought it was just more of his confusing voices and faces, but then it came to him. Paul Newman had given such a look to a bull at close range in *Butch Cassidy and the Sundance Kid.* The Frenchman was mocking him! It was beyond the imagination. He had not known the French to be fans of Paul Newman. And the Frenchman was not even careful to pretend to be curious about the burglary. He wasn't curious, obviously, because he knew about it! You do not say "the burglary" and have normal, innocent people just sit there. It was the best evidence he had that the Frenchman was the very person of large size his cheerful wife was walking hill and dale to find, and this explained why she had been seen near them all day. It was fantastic, but Mario had become the paid escort to the man his wife was leaving him for, and all day he had been keeping the man just out of her reach. It was too much. "It just goes to show you," Mario said aloud to no one in particular. "In this world, one word says it all." He had heard this useful line from an American baseball player of Latin extraction. The ballplayer had actually said, "In America, one word says it all," but Mario figured if one word said it all, it said it all wherever you were. If there was such a thing as universality, this logic was sound. He wished the ballplayer had gone on to say what the word that said it all was.

Mario planned to strike the Frenchman, but he was going to have to be careful that the Frenchman did not somehow survive the blow and sit on him. *Large size* was actually an inadequate description of the Frenchman. He was *mozzafiato*—take your breath away.

"Jerry Lewis is not an international comic genius," Mario announced suddenly and loudly. At this, both Germano and Adriano Buffala stood up and assumed crouched positions not unlike runners before the start of long-distance races. But the Frenchman, who had been rummaging briefly in the toolshed beside the hospitality patio, waved Mario off with a gesture of impatience. He emerged from the shed with a shovel, and after quartering about the patio a bit came to a spot he seemed to find significant, and with all his weight sank the shovel into the ground. He stood on the flush tangs of the shovel with a look on his face knowing and confident. Germano and Adriano took off, and Mario casually strolled to his Fiat before firing it up and making haste away from the advanced Frenchman and the vineyard full of stories.

Mario had no idea how to contend with a large Frenchman who did not care if you insulted Jerry Lewis. The idea even frightened him a little. One might as well be dealing with a Moroccan, or worse. A Frenchman unprepared to defend Jerry Lewis might do anything at all, because he would be a man who was empty inside, perhaps not even a man in the normal sense but a kind of alien—an *anti-homme*, as he thought the French might put it.

Mario's imagination was not equal to the prospect of the empty Frenchman. A non-Jerry-Lewis-loving frog gave him chills, in fact. He rolled up the cab's windows and had a calming talk with Cicciolina, whose *tette*—if it were possible—had, since the day before, assumed an aspect of greater lift, greater heaviness, greater size. She was a marvel, *l'onorevole* Cicciolina, and he was gladdened at that moment to be a modern Italian. It gave you a sense of well-being to have one of your own kind in high places. In a way, though not in an entirely rational way, it was not unlike having your mother run the country. It was like turning the country into a home, a home into a bed, a bed into a passion of large size.

Mario discovered his wife at table before a plate of steaming pasta. She looked undisturbed, serene, even— if you could imagine it—happy. That was like her. She had the most developed capacity for self-delusion of any woman Mario had ever known.

She was even wearing house slippers. Thus she had thought to take off and conceal whatever kind of magical running shoes she had worn for the day's incalculable mileage. She spoke pleasantly to Mario, who waved her off and searched the house thoroughly for these supernatural shoes.

In the course of his search, he located, in his nightstand drawer where he always kept it, his black address book, which contained the ninety-five names and numbers of his girlfriends. Some of these, Mario admitted, were untried. He had copied them from the secret rosters of local convents. It was absurd to just write all these girls off because they were pursuing a celibate life. Not all of them would become nuns, some would necessarily fall by the wayside, and these girls would be fresh and full of desire. It was like kinetic and potential energy, if you wanted to be scientific about it. Mario's notebook was a trove of potential female energy. The notebook was where it had always been, and where it had *not* been the night before, following the burglary. His wife, for some odd reason, must have taken it with her on her failed, foolish quest for larger size.

He seized the book and intended to confront her with it, and with the absurd note she'd left about his not knowing beans about large size. He would walk into the steamy, happy kitchen full of her weird fantasy and slap both of these documents on the table and tell her that her fantastic lack of sense was at an end.

But he could not locate the note, and the address book alone did not somehow seem sufficient. A notebook of ninety-five girlfriends' numbers presented defiantly to a wife seemed vaguely not the perfect thing. It spoke of the kind of damning evidence presented by one side in a court of law that eventually somehow works to the advantage of the other. He left the notebook in the drawer. He would get Cicciolina's number and that would make it ninety-six.

He sat down to eat with his wife, who served him cheerfully. She was a marvel of deceit. She then had the temerity to ask him how his day had gone.

"You are fantastic," he told her.

"Thank you, Mario." She blushed. *She blushed.* In their previous, honest life together, she always blushed

when he complimented her, and here she was counter-
feiting the same complex physiological response. Anyone
who could do that, under circumstances of running off
for larger size, was worthy of Hollywood in Mario's opinion. Or was crazy. She was either as good as Katharine
Hepburn or she was gone. Either way, he had lost his
wife. It was perfect, a situation that made perfect sense:
he was sitting across from his smiling wife, who had fixed
them an excellent meal and was solicitous of him and
his petty workday, and he was smiling back, and anybody
looking in their windows—as Mario certainly now knew
people with black hearts did—would think them happily
wed. But the party with the black heart could not see
that his smiling wife had said he knew no beans about
large size and had spent a night and a day running around
cheerfully looking for it and had lost her mind.

Mario ate normally, the food was her best (wouldn't
it be?), and they retired and had a relationship in which
his wife was especially ardent (wouldn't she be?), and
Mario forced himself to satisfy her. But he plotted
throughout the relationship (it took some time, because
his size did not want to be really large—how could it?)
to go the following day to see Sevriano Buffala about his
wife. He distrusted psychiatry—in his view you were
either crazy or you weren't, like pregnancy—but he loved
the person who had *been* his wife, and it was worth
pursuing the fantasy of modern medicine for the chance
of bringing her back to earth.

The instability of the human mind, its unsteady
footing and proclivity to slide down avalanches of delu-
sion, was the thing about human life that most disturbed
Mario. Famine, war, genocide, birth defects, violent
crime, racism, bad automobiles—all these things paled

next to mental instability for Mario. It was a shame. It was one thing not to be able to eat, or to get shot, or to be born with something missing, or to have a car not start, but not to know what was up was incalculably worse. Hell, Mario thought, was precisely that—not having a clue about what was up. He felt so sorry for his departed wife that, when her ardor had receded, he indulged in uncharacteristic sentimentality and kissed her on the forehead. So dire was her state, she appeared grateful.

In the night Mario dreamed of having to return to the vineyard to pick up the Frenchman. There he found Germano and Adriano haggardly standing beside the supine form of the advanced Frenchman. Beside him was a four-foot-deep hole and beside that a mound of dirt. Checking instinctively and furtively, Mario could detect no exposed spolia of tombs or parts of mummies, and the dirt did not look radioactive.

Germano said that they were lucky. The Frenchman had dug between tombs. Had he simply pulled up an active, large vine, he would have gotten a mummy. Adriano showed Mario his eight crossed fingers, which he had held crossed by sitting on them all the while the Frenchman had dug, and which now hurt him considerably to undo. "That was foolish," Mario said. "You could hurt yourself, and what is more, my needle valve is sticking on the way out here, and you are the best at a needle valve. Can you look at it in your condition?" Adriano unwound his fingers and checked them in the air, and they went to take a look at Mario's carburetor, leaving the Frenchman in his fat, snoring peace.

Then Mario had a frightening dream. He dreamed that none of his previous day and night had taken place, that it had all been itself some kind of dream. His wife had missed him because he had come home much later than usual, delayed by the officer, and she had gone ruefully to bed alone. She was in the bed when he searched the house but was concealed in the covers. In his search for stolen valuables he had read not a note from her but one of the open passages about modern Italy and the modern Italian. This dream was unnerving.

Mario had no capacity for multiple levels of illusion, for the kind of layered reality that a dream like this suggested. He began to sweat and toss in now partial sleep, and then the dream sweetened back into things familiar— he and Adriano and Germano were adjusting the needle valve. He calmed down. As soon as his sleep was regular, however, the dream turned on him again. As Adriano reached in to turn the valve, the needle somehow became the gap in the front teeth of Sevriano Buffala, the psychiatrist, whose smiling face, which suddenly resembled the face of Sigmund Freud himself, looked at him from under the hood of the taxi. The face spoke to him: "It's *you* who's crazy, Mario Moscalini. Your wife is a rock of salt."

This all made perfect sense, in the dream. Dreams have a way of doing that. Needle valves can look like gaps in teeth, and people being rocks of salt can be perfectly sensible. Mario sat up in bed and marveled at the lunacies he had just accepted as reason.

When he got up the next morning he decided to postpone his trip to see Sevriano Buffala. He was not really worried that the doctor of bogus science would actually attempt to suggest that the trouble was with him. It was just that maybe he was acting a bit precipitously in taking his wife to see the smiling quack. It was the kind of innocent, well-meaning thing people did all the time in the interest of their loved ones—and sometimes never saw them again. The loved ones went straight into lifelong loony bins. The risks of being irresponsible in matters of unhinged relatives were very high. You had to think twice, or three times, about just how deranged they were. His wife was not, after all, *dangerous* to anyone, including herself. She had not interfered with his seeing Cicciolina, which at present was what *really* mattered to him, so why force her to walk a shaman's tightrope of mental fitness?

Besides, if he went directly out to the vineyard this morning to catch Sevriano, the chances were extremely high that Germano and Adriano would force him into filling in the Frenchman's hole. Or worse, if the Frenchman had expired from his august labor, they might make him party to the burial, which might get tedious later in a legal sense if the Michelin company proved attached to their scribe and sent authorities. It would look suspicious, the Buffala brothers and a respected taxi driver burying a fat man in a hole he himself had dug. And his disinterment would rattle the Buffala brothers to no end, for fear that mummies, vipers, aphrodisiacs, or nuclear fuel waste might be discovered. Any of that and their vineyard was probably at an end. On top of all this, Mario did not want to develop trouble with his needle valve on the drive out there.

He got quietly up and repaired to the kitchen and decided to surprise his wife by fixing breakfast for them. She was sleeping late. She deserved it—it could not be more obvious that she was under considerable strain and needed all the rest she could get.

Mario was a little rusty in the kitchen, but he was confident he could remember his good mother's recipe for *pizza bianca*, and he wanted to cook the bread in the old wood stove his wife never used. He liked the smell of bread most when it was cooked over wood. It made bread taste like some kind of airy game.

He set about rolling the ingredients for the pizza together on his wife's floured board and soon had a large round of dough that was kneadable in the extreme. He vaguely remembered that the pizza did not want a lot of kneading, because it became tough, but the mound beneath his working hands began to feel good to him. A little more, he decided. As he worked the dough, a sensation of excitement came into his size, and another sensation crept up the back of his neck, as if he were being watched. He wanted to turn to see who was watching him, but the mound of dough held him. He had to work it a little more. It was absurd, but the heavy slag of leavening bread reminded him not a little of Cicciolina's ample *tette*, or one of them, anyway. He caressed her, forming her up to him, then mashing her gently, pressing her entire *tetta* to her chest with both his hands. He would have bent to kiss her but for the absolute need to see who was watching him. You do not kiss the *tetta* of *l'onorevole* Cicciolina on a board in the kitchen if someone is watching you. For a second—very brief, but disturbing—the flattened dough then resembled not Cicciolina but a piece of the hide of the white, advanced Frenchman.

Before he turned, he decided the party watching him could not be his wife—she was still soundly asleep. It was probably the prowler, the burglar. This gave him a thrill. Maybe he should continue to caress Cicciolina until the man was closer to him, and then suddenly whirl and strike the bastard a mortal blow with an iron fist that had but a second before been an incredibly tender, loving hand. This had much appeal.

He waited but could not hear the blackguard crossing the kitchen. It was more than a little unsettling to try to hear someone creep up on you as you worked up pizza bianca on a floury board in your kitchen. Finally it occurred to Mario that he might be in some marginal danger, and it was certain that he was not—distracted as he was—acquitting himself well with Cicciolina. He took a deep breath and whirled. No one was there. What he saw where he had expected the man—it was crazy, but he now realized he had expected the Frenchman—was a Michelin guide to Italy open to the psalm of the modern Italian. He looked at the book. He stared it down. It was on its back, and across the room, yet somehow was watching him. If he thought a book on its back could watch him, maybe he should see Sevriano Buffala after all.

He kindled up a small fire in the old stove and found a pan for Cicciolina's dear bread. She felt, she smelled, so good it was incredible. Mario was salivating. He thought to surprise his wife with an even larger surprise than breakfast prepared by a respectable taxi driver. He put Cicciolina in the oven and, before going to the bedroom, tossed the Michelin guide to Italy in the firebox. Cicciolina could use the heat. When Mario served the tough bread to his wife she seemed not to notice. She seemed warmed by his gesture and ate the pizza smiling at him girlishly, as if, it seemed to him, he had been away for a long time and they were consequently a little new and exciting to each other, as they had been years before. His wife sat in bed eating the bread and deftly picking up crumbs from her bosom with a moist finger and looking at him when she put the crumbs in her mouth, and Mario sat looking seriously back at her, thinking, It is like I have been away somewhere.

Dr. Ordinary

[**D**r. Ordinary found solace in nothing. He found his shoes untied during surgery. He found his mother once, when she was in her sixties, naked in the bathtub calling for a fresh martini. He found bluebirds too far south. He found pies too sweet to eat. He found God with no difficulty, but locating his belief another matter.

He found it curious that he should have gone to medical school in the first place. He found a human head in the car trunk of his anatomy-class partner. He found, after his certain initial horror, that it was not the head of the cadaver he shared with his ghoulish roommate.

He found Tuesday the most trying day of the week, by far. He found a stray dog. He found a wallet full of cash. He found a lost child on the edge of a huge mall parking lot. He found it difficult to turn her in without coming under the suspicion of authority. He found telling them he was a doctor to be of no help.

He found beautiful—as beautiful as crystals and snowflakes and precious gems—the cysts and stones and lumps he took from human bodies. He found dry cleaning to be tantamount to not cleaning. He found he had no objection to staples in clothes, but he could not abide them in paper.

He found whiners offensive. He found a rare buffalo nickel in his pant cuff. He found blues-singers-in-Angola shows on TV totally absorbing. He found the behavior of mature people unpredictable. He found the doctrine of Christian charity at once commendable and absurd.

He found women close to tears at all times. He found old-fashioned foundation ads such as those in the Sears catalogue more titillating than modern-day pictures of nudes. He found relief in tension and none in release. He found certain sentimental poems, of the sort found on greeting cards, salacious. He found that if, as he gave a woman a physical examination of any intimate region, she spoke to him *loudly*, he was attracted to her strongly. He found impossible the notion of taking sexual advantage of a patient.

He found color-gradient charts at paint stores the most engaging art he had ever seen, and he had the world's largest, if not only, collection of them. He found mules and other sterile hybrids, excepting sterile hybrid plants, most sympathetic. He found vegetarians everywhere.

He found Campbell's soups odious in the extreme,

more risky to consume than a Coke with a rat in the bottle. He found himself sometimes longing for the fine and light linen of yesteryear—white suits and handmade doilies. He found his relatives no more boring a lot than anyone else finds his. He found salvation in loss. He found cheer in the lugubrious carrying-on of patients who thought themselves incorrectly to be dying.

He found photographs of landscape pretentious. He found altar architecture rude. He found fresh-faced waitresses the most likely to spit in food about to be served. He found no difficulty, in principle, in pederasty, though he found no impulse for it in himself.

He found coloring with crayons an art form worthy of adults. He found fast cars on TV somehow more offensive than fast cars in person. He found reptiles of all forms pitiful. He found expensive tools harder to lose than cheap tools, to his surprise. He found telephone solicitation not so much annoying as vaguely rakish, if not prurient. He found pretty certain kinds of . . . of nothing.

He found himself a pallbearer at his own funeral, and the strongest of the six. He found himself less moved by his demise than anyone. He found, when touching the expensive, pointless, fake-brass coffin, that he had made the largest mistake of his life in allowing himself to be put in it. He found no solace in regret, but he regretted not willing himself, unembalmed, into a simple wooden box made not by a funereal concern but by a cabinetmaker. He found this sentiment repulsively common, but he found it to be true, deep, and his.

He found himself, once dead, able to relive his life with free editorial rein. He found the possibilities for revision endless. He found he had no interest in changing a thing. He found it easier to conceive of an alteration for the worse than one for the better. Dead, he found his clothes better fitting and longer wearing. He found this both reasonable, most reasonable, and odd.

General Rancidity

I   General Rancidity ran the obstacle course and the whorehouse. He ran away from nothing. He ran to weight on furlough. He ran headlong into marriage. He ran aground once in a ten-foot dinghy in a foot of water, disposing himself toward a career in the infantry.

He ran religious seekers out of his unit, and out of the Army if he could. "Bullets and Jesus do not mix" ran his slogan on this policy. The devout consequently ran scared before him, scattering like small fish before the large pagan shadow that General Rancidity was.

He ran underground raffles for military contraband, profits running into the thousands. He ran the flag up on his base personally. He ran into a woman with a jeep. He carried her fireman-style to the infirmary. Of the expression "Still waters run deep," General Rancidity said, "*Blanks*. Still water just sits there." He was much more fond of the expression "Fell off a turnip truck." He wanted no one accusing him of having fallen off a turnip truck. Consequently, he ran a tight ship.

He ran into difficulties, over time, with his friends— they ran off and left him. He was resigned to it: with familiarity, his turdy behavior around and his ungracious treatment of his friends increased until the general index of rancidity in his character exceeded the practical limits that people, even soldiers, were designed, or desired, to put up with. Only the truly rancid themselves could run with General Rancidity for long, and the truly rancid were rare.

One day General Rancidity, running late, ran low on gas and in fact ran out. No one would stop and pick him up. Thousands of lower-ranking men passed him on the roadside, running afoul of military as well as human protocol. General Rancidity's blood ran more than hot.

He ran for a period toward the officers' club, where he ran up a giant tab, to have a drink before initiating procedures to court-martial the entire base. Luck was running low, or high, depending upon your affection for General Rancidity: he was run over by the woman he had run into and carried fireman-style to the infirmary. She hit and ran.

General Rancidity's obituary ran to less than twenty-five words, the result of a twenty-five-words-or-less contest run by his best surviving friends:

> General Rancidity and the turnip truck he
> rode in on ran off the edge of the earth
> last Thursday, rancid turnips, rancid gen-
> eral, and all.

Spirits on base were running high, most high, and weather fair, and all schedules on time, and all probabilities true. Soldiers, and small schools of fish in the golf-course water hazards, ran over shoal and dale, rejoicing, relieved, relying on the base without General Rancidity to most happily, most trottingly, run itself.

Mr. Nefarious

[**M**r. Nefarious smiled, and only when smiling was he able to do anything else. When smiling he could also do nothing, but when not smiling he could do nothing but not smile. He smiled as he scissored tiny stray threads from his clothes, smiled marveling at *how many* stray threads there were, almost . . . well, enough that you wondered how many non-stray threads were in position holding the garment together rather than . . . straying off, hanging off and out of seams like . . . *flopping* around on his clothes, loose cannons on the deck of haberdashery; he smiled and snipped and snipped and there was no end, logically—he kept cutting, smiling, cut a pair of pants to pieces.

He smiled phoning a girl who was in no sense his girlfriend, or anyone's girlfriend; in fact, if you asked anyone who knew her, say even a tall woodsman type of fellow in his woodshop or on his horse how to get to this girl's house, he was supposed to know because she had been supposed to be his (the woodsman's) girlfriend once but of course wasn't, only in her mind was she, for two minutes, he (the woodsman) said, "We went out four times and she wanted to get married," and if Mr. Nefarious asked how to get to her house of the woodsman who had declined the fifth date on grounds of risk, the woodsman would say, Sure you want to go to her house? And Mr. Nefarious would smile and say, Not *her* house, I'm looking for that girl lives *near* her house, and actually both Mr. Nefarious and the woodsman would be smiling at this point, but Mr. Nefarious would smile longer, which would irritate the woodsman, and decide to phone the woman instead of risk going to her house—the tall practical fellow who could rip trees in his spare time was right.

So phoning her he smiled but when she did not answer he smiled and hung up.

Tossing a tennis ball for his dog he could smile for a quarter of an hour, all the dog and the ball could take, the dog fat and the ball a tennis ball, made for clay courts, made for concrete courts, not made for ivory and saliva courts.

He could look at bilge water and smile.

He smiled rarely at his mother.

The girl whose house the woodsman recommended they avoid reminded him of his mother, when she, the girl, smiled. When his mother smiled, she, his mother, reminded him of his childhood. When it came to his childhood there was no smiling. It seemed to him an era as humanly distant and crude as the Cro-Magnon's. If he said something stank in this era of cave dwelling, his mother corrected him: it didn't *stink*, it *smelled*. Okay, he'd assent, something *smells*, Mom, upon which she'd instruct him: "Look on your upper *lip!*" with a superior sneering tone that stopped him in his childhood tracks. *That's* the way it was in this life? Nothing stank, it *smelled*, and it was always, if you smelled it, on your own lip. Even though it was his own, this motherhood struck him as odd.

Once, he had invited a girl to swim in the family pool after school, and they had spent a fine afternoon of it together, the girl barely constrained by her two-piece and the young Mr. Nefarious dog-paddling his nose into her breasts, occasionally sinking from the cumbersome weight and bulk of his teenage tumescence, rescued each time by the girl, who breathed life back into him with a peck of a kiss and released him to paddle upstream some more. When his mother uncovered this tryst she prohibited any more on the grounds that they had been unchaperoned (obviously, the young Mr. Nefarious thought to himself), and that, therefore, the neighbors would talk.

Everywhere they went, they sued all the neighbors first thing, but in this one instance his mother had a point. They had not yet sued any. Behind them was the mother of a hoodlum who lived in juvenile detention centers, to the side of them the people who'd sold them their house and held the mortgage and had a severely retarded child, across the street a millionaire who lived abroad, next to him ever-changing renters, next to them a man who had sired thirteen children out of his one, lame, eighty-pound wife. There was no one to sue. But they would talk. To whom, he could not guess.

The young Mr. Nefarious stood there that day following his pool tryst, still marginally priapic and limping slightly from his afternoon of unrelieved water ballet, ready to assent to this absurd prohibition because he did not know if his seminiferous system could take another four-hour throttling, when his mother pulled out another stop on the organ of her rectitude. "I want you to write me," she intoned, smoking a cigarette and having her first cocktail, "an essay on *integrity*."

"On what?"

"On IN TEG RIT TEE. Do you know what integrity is?"

"Think so," the young Mr. Nefarious managed. "If not, I'll look it up."

"Good."

"Do you think it's in the *World Book*?"

He cannot remember if he actually made the last crack, only hope, and he does not remember looking up the word in the dictionary, but thinks he did, aiming to kill twenty-five words by copying the definition into his "essay," which he did not—this much is for sure—ever write. Nor did his mother ask for it. It was clear to Mr. Nefarious, if not to her, that the matter of integrity between them was extinct.

When he thought of the girl whom the woodsman recommended they all avoid, smiling and looking like his mother, he suffered a wicked thrill and then shuddered and hung up the phone before she could possibly answer it. This was a dangerous moment for Mr. Nefarious. The next thought was invariably this: everyone looks something like his, Mr. Nefarious's, mother, if you get right down to it, including himself. How could you go about life avoiding everyone on earth, and yourself, because humans resemble each other? The long-term answer to this question had worked itself out over time without his knowing it: dogs were safe, as were all people who demonstrated a total want of, or an aggressive dislike for, *integrity*. Those were your playmates in this tough world: dogs and people with shit on their upper lip. Mr. Nefarious had developed his nearly incessant smile by attempting to look at his lip.

At trees no smiling unless there was axing, and then the smiling was worked quickly into a determined slit-of-purpose mouth. But spiritually still a smile.

He smiled writing letters to people, overintimate, unsolicited revelations of himself, and smiled retrieving from the mailbox mail-order catalogues mostly from fancy gardening-tool concerns, in each of which was an outdoor bench costing not less than $500. To X, a woman who certainly had never been in any sense his girlfriend but who had been for damned sure somebody's girlfriend, namely Charles's, to whom she had been securely married for fifteen years or more, he wrote, "I do not customarily"—here he smiled—"write love letters," and then he saved the day, which made his smile dim, or curl, ever so rancidly, by of course not declaring his love for her, which did not really exist anyway (he smiled: where, with whom, *on* whom, *did* it exist?), saved the day by just letting the letter drift off into a rather lame and nonspecific lament about his . . . not *depression*, just *downness*, all of which was designed—he smiled— to suggest he did love her, about 23 percent. That was enough love and at the correct angle to come at a married woman with better sense than to listen to garbage—she could certainly not entertain 25 percent, a full one-quarter throttle—and Mr. Nefarious smiled, sealed it up, stamped it with two stamps (one was extra so he could lick twice), packed it off in his country mailbox, raising the red flag, and wondered on the way back from the mailbox what it would be like to have—it bordered on not smiling to think of it—a $598.95 teak bench sitting out in the rain, the rain, and then the sun.

Mr. Desultory

[**M**r. Desultory cannot, for the life of him, or of anyone else, or of any *thing*, do *this* after *that*, or *that* after *this*, if either sequence might logically look sequential from a distance of, say, 2 cm or more. Mr. Desultory, as a somewhat colorful British roofer he once knew put it, referring not to Mr. Desultory but to the roofing concern in whose employ they at the moment were, Mr. Desultory an ordinary interloper and the colorful Brit somewhat more wayward in that he had accepted a proposal of marriage from an unnubile American woman to stay his imminent deportation only to find himself *praying* for deportation immediately after the honeymoon and thereafter referring to his immigration bride as the Dragon—anyway the colorful British roofer subject to a harridaning beyond the wildest torments of immigration authorities or coal mining or whatever he had to do back home, it must have been something unpleasant for the Dragon Knot, as the wedding was called, to have been tied in the first place, though even Mr. Desultory can remember the colorful British roofer's having said she, the Dragon, was "sweet," he used that word, and straight, without a glint of irony or sarcasm in his glinty little eyes, all colorful British roofers have glinty little eyes to match their glinty little Cockney mouths, where are we? The Cockney married to the sweet, fat (he said she was *huge,* a matter that all the boys on the roof found impossible to verify, though try they did—running to the edge of the roof when the Dragon came to retrieve her husband, and looking down from their roof at the roof of the tiny car from which she never stepped and speculating just how large she might be to be in so small a car, what is that a Comet or what? She can't be *that* big, and look at old Bob stepping right on in, he step in there without a shoehorn, don't he? Don't see him squoze out the window either—look, he *smilin!*) American girl, the Cockney married to the American girl told her that the company for whom he and Mr. Desultory and those who speculated upon her size worked could not have organized a piss-up in a brewery or a shaggin session in a brothel, and it is arguable that both colorful expressions, which had to be translated somewhat to American idiom, both expressions could be said to apply, and to *have* applied, though not so much then as now, for he is worse now, to Mr. Desultory himself.

Mr. Desultory cannot rub two quarters—not quarters, ideas, he can't get two . . . *things,* he can't *do* two related, sequential, yes it is in sequencing that . . . *this* goes before *that,* so he'll get *that* squared away and then go to do *this,* but it is already backwards, he must do this *then* that, so forget *that*, let's do *this* now, but *this* could arguably precede *this* which is already *that* because here's this new this here—two quarters refers to wealth, or lack of it, a tired little phrase that must have come from the Depression, a time which sometimes Mr. Desultory feels sounds like his kind of time. He could have handled the Great Depression, you either jumped out of a skyscraper window, no sequencing problem there: *one* open her up, *two* review at the last minute your collapsed financial state, weep and moil your hands shedding tears, ink running on your last financial statement—maybe not ink but pencil, would a last financial statement, even one coming to zeros zeros zeros, be in ink or pencil?

Is it ink or pencil? In the Depression did your accountant hold behind his back your last big ledger sheet and smile because maybe he did not like you and then whip out the pale-green Boorum & Pease ten-column double-entry ledger sheet and—did they have . . . was Boorum & Pease extant in the thirties? Or in '29, rather? You'd think, wouldn't you, that of all businesses to go out with the lights it would have been first and foremost, very head of the line, some outfit making accounting products, zero dollars after all does not require extensive books, so if Boorum & Pease existed before the Crash it had to have Crashed, it was therefore born from the embers, later, its gentle green products sprouting humbly up along with other, new, and miraculous shoots of recovery, the accountant could not whip out Boorum & Pease paper and you couldn't wonder then or now if it was pen or pencil that sent you flying out the window, the good old double-hung sash window with two fine slugs, or pendula, what's the right word, those long, hangy-down doobers on the rope inside the walls, iron, like billy sticks, hard to find now, very hard to find, hard to know what to do with them if you do find one, tell other people who are looking for them for whatever reason they're looking for them that you've found one, or ten, maybe ten is enough to get them to buy them from you, then they go get some old windows, wind up fixing up a house of about Depression vintage—can you jump out of the window fifty years before the damned pig-iron thingamajigs are to be used restoring perhaps the same window? Can you jump? Is it an inked or penciled zero, whether on Boorum & Pease or not (let's forget that absurd debate!), is it a zero . . . or maybe a *negative* . . . yes, why on earth would a zero inspire anyone to jump out of a window? Zeros never hurt anyone, it's *negative numbers* make people kill themselves, zeros are perfectly harmless, often salubrious, just sometimes unsettling to the capitalist mind with its impractical insistence on constant growth, a more absurd proposition than the Boorum & Pease wrangle by a factor of . . . of a lot, so is it an *inked* negative million dollars which will keep your kids from attending college, which wasn't so important in 1930 anyway, they could just go to your alma mater, the School of Hard Knocks, but a negative million dollars would keep your wife out of the beauty parlor and good-looking probably low-cut post-flapper dresses, and you out of walnut-wainscoted boardrooms for the rest of your bathtub-gin life, or is it a *penciled* negative million dollars that could be erased and changed either before you jump out the window or, if you take yourself by the scrotum and leap, *after* you jump out the window—

   —Mr. Desultory can't jump out the window in his

beloved simple time, no binary easy time that, a debit-credit St. Vitus dance before a skyscraper window; the Depression's not for him, maybe something earlier, wax seals come to mind, quill pens and ink, no, not more ink, trouble there, before *writing* would be safer, rocks, fires, elephants, and not elephants that evoke global economic ecologic politics ivory wars Greenpeace ozone acid rain what to do what to do what to do, no, elephants and plenty of them, maybe more than you want to see, but let's leave that alone, impossible idea *surplus herd* in ancient times, elephants, plenty of them, yes: elephants with hair on them, don't even have to call them elephants if they have hair on them, or *enough* hair, all elephants have hair, bristles coming out of their deep rubber flesh like *wire*—how much hair was the cutting-off point, made you a mastodon, cut the girls as it were from the boys, sheep from goats, dainty modern pachyderm from the woolly mammoth?

Mr. Desultory must continue to regress, it won't work, he can go all the way to the Big Bang and still not manage two consecutive or consequential—no, just sequential, two . . . okay: Big Bang. BANG! Is Mr. Desultory in it or not in it? Does he go *that* way into the black hole, whatever that is and if one may enter it, or *this* way into the light of day, elephants with or without hair, Boorum & Pease in ink or pencil, windows to be jumped out of or to be restored—here, perhaps, his error, or not his, somebody's, Fate's or Accident's: if he had gone *that* way, through the black hole at the beginning of time, at the moment before which there was no decision but after which there was no deciding, he would not be in the difficulties he is in today. There would be no problem. It, the Bang, was a larger, simpler, if in a sense higher window than the later double-hung one in the Depression, and he wishes he had jumped, or been sucked, through it.

Almost.

Nonprofit

[**F**rom a line of famous men I am, and of armoire and men I sing, and my father doesn't have a goddamned thing to do with it.

My coffee cup leaks! The girl, if you think she'd check to see if the cups leak at the takeout. No. And walk eight blocks without noticing, without the cup falling through the bag. If my father *had* a goddamned thing to do with it, he doesn't *now,* and I'd like to see the bastard who will say it to my face.

An excellent wool blazer contravenes the wit of planned obsolescence to the utmost. An excellent wool blazer nearly obviates, forever, the *new* wool blazer. Do *you* think my father had a goddamned thing to do with it? I don't even think *his* father had a goddamned thing to do with it. *The Wall Street Journal* may well be an excellently written paper but I do not find it helpful. It is of marginal use to me. I don't care for it. I don't care to be *buzzed*, either. We can, if we want to, stem the tide of technological tackiness, we can have the girl just get up and knock and lean in, or present herself with dignity and inform you that someone wishes to speak with you on the string and Dixie cup. What is so wrong with *that*? Do you think I'd stay here if my father had a goddamned thing to do with it? Stay? Remain? Hold prideless untenable sinecure when of I sing . . . really, there's nothing wrong with *lineage*, that is how you win the Kentucky Derby and the *only* way you win the Kentucky Derby—if my father had a goddamned thing to do with it I'll eat . . . Mister Donut here, I'll eat that box of Mister Donut. She got the white, choke you to death you breathe wrong, High-Level Corporate Exec Dies of Inhaling 10X Confectioner's Sugar, *Wall Street Journal*, page 6. If my father *had* a goddamned thing to do with it, it's water over the bridge now, spilled milk under the dam. Anybody who tells you he did is a high-water asshole who's jealous. How *could* he have had a goddamned thing to do with it if I tied his shoes for him, in the end? When you tie an old man's shoes, he does not have a goddamned thing to do with it. Not a *god*damned thing.

There are times in my life when I wonder what is the struggle for, what is the sacrifice all about. There are considerations beyond the simple and obvious question of why are we nonprofit. They go deeper than that. They go all the way to the foundation of altruism itself. I wonder about that. I seriously pause some days—is it worth it? If there was a *shade* of truth that my father, whom I see to this day in his pajamas and untied shoes ready for me to get him ready for a board meeting, too embarrassed to have anyone but me know, had a goddamned thing to do with it I'd quit, naturally, quickly spontaneously and combustively with vigor dispatch and hortatory glory of distinguished men from good clubs and better backgrounds breeding will out, out, out, he had not a thing to do with a thing, not a whit with a whit, or I'm a monkey's uncle, and I'm not a monkey's uncle.

Miss Jacobs, please come get this coffee mess off my desk, prepare to retrieve lunch, Russian dressing on roast beef, and inspect the cups well before you take one step toward this office bearing liquids of any kind, is that clear, is it understood, is it *clearly understood*?

On thin ice, Miss Jacobs, *Mizz* Jacobs, her predecessor having had the misfortune to abuse the string and Dixie cup and be overheard remarking "gives the air of a man perpetually emerging from a barbershop" (she had literary aspirations, I'm afraid)—I asked who has the air of a perpetual emergent from a tonsorial parlor and she *blushed*. You understand. Let her go, let her go, let her go. Had to, had to, had to.

Miss Resignation

Lisa smoked her first Bingo card un-
noticed. She coughed, coughed considerably, but not as
much as one might expect smoking cardboard, and her
condo neighbors could hear her coughing through the
walls, but it sounded not unlike their own rheumy hack-
ing and gasping and they never fathomed she had taken
to smoking her Bingo cards. She never *won* at Bingo and
the decision to smoke the losing cards—not just burn
them—was a deep, involuted response to her lack of luck.

She had a mynah bird that did not talk and that had
lost so many feathers to his ineradicable mite problem
that he looked more like a desert lizard than a bird.

Her refrigerator would regularly fail to close by one-
quarter of an inch, which was enough to perish the per-
ishable and the compressor.

Her curtain rods sagged in the middle so badly that
her drapes slid from the sides of her windows into the
middle of the span.

One day four of forty hair curlers refused to let go and she had to use scissors to get them out.

She had a beautiful daughter.

She could no longer effect a long-distance phone call.

The television one day blinked and then showed her a tiny, shrinking, green pupil in the middle of the dark screen. The repairman, whom she secured by yelling at as he drove down the street, said he could not fix her set.

"Why not?" she asked.

"It's tubes," he said.

Potatoes were a staple of her diet. One day she experimented with how potatoes bounce on linoleum. They bounce pretty well and are not damaged much.

Toast impressed her as a waste of time. Bread was *already* cooked; you eat it or you do not.

Socks, likewise, seemed superfluous, if one has shoes.

She liked football and was *absolutely certain* that she could have been an excellent off-tackle slant-type power runner in a wishbone or two-back set. 44 was her number.

Forty-four was her bra size, too. This had held her back in life, she felt.

The salt air outside had corroded the aluminum frames of her windows to the point she was afraid to open them for fear of not being able to close them. They, the frames, had little white pocks on them, reminiscent of chenille.

Under her sink was a rattrap she could not set, for her nerves, and a rat. She baited the trap for him and fed him, safely and humanely, from the harmless little copper bait seesaw. She wondered if the rat knew *she* knew the trap was just a . . . just a whatever a sprung trap you continue to bait is. Perhaps he thought it a rather cruel thing to do, or maybe he got a kick out of it, or maybe he just ate the cheese, period. It was hard to know what a rat thought. Once, she put a small wad of wet toilet paper on the bait seesaw and he ate that, too, or at least took it off somewhere with him. All in all, she thought of him as a good sport, a good sport under the sink, and took comfort in it. She resisted the idea that he ate in fear, held his breath before biting the cheese. But she resisted equally the notion of feeding him on a saucer instead of the little bait seesaw—that was openly feeding a rat. He was not a dog. The rat under the sink was not a dog. The rat under the sink who could eat on a guillotine and find a use for or even eat toilet paper was not a dog. You could discover what a dog did with toilet paper, wet or dry. A dog is no rat. The rat is in possession of a dignity of desperation, and not *the* dignity of desperation, for there are many dignities of desperation. There is the desperate dignity of smoking the Bingo card which represents your millionth consecutive loss at Bingo, which is not even a true gamble. There is the desperate dignity of sweltering in your apartment with its closed windows because the event of window-frame failure, caused by electrolytical erosion of aluminum, will admit of the whole, giant ocean but blocks away and of all the destructive power of the sea, its swallowed cargoes and lives and lighthouse failures and fogs and seas higher than ships and icebergs and scurvy and sailors spreading syphilis and the entire trunk of doom that is Davy Jones's locker two blocks away. This is just one of hundreds of desperations of dignity, not opening your windows.

A dog may have dignity, but not a desperate dignity. No dog, save those very first ones to perceive the domestication plans, has ever been possessed of a dignity of desperation. It is arguable that the kind of poodle whose nails get painted purple by Lisa's condo neighbors can have a desperation, often betrayed by its nail-clicking dancing irrational barking skin problems self-mutilation visits to dog psychologists etc., but this, too, is not a desperation of dignity. This is clearly a desperation of *indignity*, and why Lisa likes a rat under the sink, not a dog.

Flood

[In a flood we had, a poet I know
came walking down the riverbank, just as I recovered
from the river itself a woman—I was in it grabbing the
good things a flood can bring, which might sound a bit
dangerous but isn't, really, if you place yourself on a
sandbar, as I had, or in an eddy closer to the bank, as
had a buddy of mine who'd come over to drink beer and
watch the flood with me until we decided to get *in* it and
grab loot—the poet asked me (and I know he was able
to see that I was holding what he had to perceive as a
drowned woman, he could see her back, broad and pale,
as she rose up out of the dark water more or less into my
arms, and I mean rather gradually and smoothly, as
though she were tipping up on her toes for a kiss, so
amorously and languidly in fact that I was not alarmed
at the immediate prospect of kissing a dead woman, in
fact the issue of her medical condition did not cross my
mind, what crossed my mind was *beauty*, which Itself I

thought I was beholding—*Beauty*—though in the upper corner of my landward eye I could see my beer buddy beginning to look alarmed, seeing me, as he was, stare without alarm into the eyes of what he also had to think was a drowned woman, *without alarm* hardly being correct, I should say without the *kind* of alarm one is expected to display in these circumstances, for I was undergoing a most profound alarm, a perhaps uncommon despair you can have if you find yourself, as I was finding myself, holding a woman so stunningly beautiful you do not even perceive that she is *wet*, let alone dead, and now I think that she was *not wet*: a heart-stopping dread comes over you that this will not last, this look she gives with her eyes that says we could have been an item, you and me, her eyes dark and a bit widened, widened you think by her precise knowledge that a huge love is possible here in all senses except the real, and you do not dare even kiss a woman in these situations for fear of somehow shortening or spoiling the little time you have, time which is already beginning to collapse as you see your beer buddy upstream starting to wade down, you can tell, to get you back to your senses, your time together which you elect to protect by letting her go back into the flood with one giant shoulder-slumping sigh of resignation before he gets there, and her flowing hair blends into the tea-colored water, and she joins the common flotsam of tires and cows and appliances and light bulbs, and your beer buddy stops, more stunned)—and the poet asked me, when she was gone, "Why is this water so dark?"

And then he asked if we saw *his* wife earlier come down the riverbank, and though we did, we did not answer, could not answer—I know of no way to answer a question like that, yet kneeling, facing upstream, with what has happened to me going downstream: in fact he requires no answer, he knows that his pallid wife is ahead of him, and not far enough ahead to be lost, and he is therefore indifferent to one's rescue, or whatever I did, with whatever I had, dead woman or mermaid. This is the notion I have, kneeling, as close to drowning the poet as he ever needs anyone to be. I know something about this uncurious poet, I can be most uncurious myself.

Before she arrived, I watched with careful indifference the baby dolls, bicycles, hair dryers (the institutional dome type—very little in a good flood makes sense), a piano with a deer on it . . . Yet what one *watches* is the water—swirls, slicks, butter-colored suds. As a consequence, women can surprise you.

I know some poets who would have leapt into the water and watched the face of this visionary woman disappear, uttering the same pained gasp I did, asking only, "Is it over—between you two?" before diving in headlong downstream after her. And some poets I know would not have asked but thrashed thigh-deep to her and taken her roughly by the hair from your very embrace.

But today's poet stays his course. "I'm not lost, am I? I don't recognize things with all this water. It sure is *dark*, too." The pallid figure of his wife lures him on, she also who walked by the magic scene.

The poet keeps going downriver. My wife, my wife, he thinks. Having asked after his living, actual wife, having seen the release of a mermaid he would not acknowledge, he now thinks about his dead, nonactual wife, his first wife.

He sees her in only a handful of fixed attitudes,

lovely aspects, doing a handful of things, dear wifely functions he was indifferent to when she was alive. His indifference to these touching scenes killed her, he thinks. Ironing.

She is ironing his shirts, humming a popular song. A top-forty radio thing. Heavy cotton broadcloth shirts she presses, working the iron like a hot trowel in mortar, and somehow the freshness of the laundered shirts transfers to her, to her dress, her dress becomes in his memory a spectacular simple girly A-line—crisp, sweet, damp—and she his wife a cool-skinned model of a girl doing all this for him, with equanimity and grace, and if he were not following her replacement down a river, not watching the water lest someone's mermaid surface and appeal to him for help, he would whistle a tune and go to his first wife and nose her in the pleats and darts as she irons, over light steam.

Kansas

[**T**he diner quit serving food, but it did not close. Likewise, the drive-in stopped showing movies but remained open. Songbirds of all character and kind gave their distinctive calls and showed their identifying profiles and markings and gave cats hell and made a general paean to Roger Tory Peterson. A lone Allis Chalmers combine dominated the skyline. It, the machine, was for sale, used, quite used.

The ladies of the town were so nice, and had been so deliberately nice all their natural lives, that they came to regard cancer as a blessing. Most of them got it; those that didn't felt cheated, left out.

The men had never learned to cuss, drink, fight, adulterate, or drive too fast. They stood there as their wives received the good bad news and as the songbirds flitted about their heads like gnats. "What a revolting development this is," one of them said, earnestly thinking the remark funny. "It's Tuesday," the comic farmer continued, "and will be all day unless it rains." He could not suppress a giggle.

It no longer bothered him that he did not know—no one knew—who the father of his wheat was. He had come, over the years, to regard his wheat not as bastard wheat but as adoptive. No one knew the father of the adopted, and that did not make for calling them bastards. "That's being *wrapped too tight*," he concluded, using for the first time, with a thrill, a line he had heard on a television comedy show he did not understand but laughed at anyway.

He had heard *flip your wig* on the same show. *Flip your wig* and another even more obscure expression used near it, *wig out*, made him uncomfortable. He told the Allis Chalmers dealer that the used combine was *wigged out*, to test the meaning. The Chalmers dealer merely shrugged and patted him on the shoulder and walked back into his showroom. He had meant that the combine was *worn out*, but now, having been a smartass, he had no idea what *wigged out* meant, and he was afraid to proof the term any further.

The diner was open but not serving food, and the drive-in let you park and put a speaker in your car but showed no movie. You passed your unused napkin back to the waitress with a very small tip, and you put the silent speaker back on its post and drove away. The world was getting easier, in its way, as it got harder to figure. People were confused somewhat, but they were losing weight and were not subject to sex and violence from Hollywood. Children were not acting confused at all, but—here was a thing to ponder—they had never been overweight, and they had never objected to sex and violence in their entertainment. Things, people felt, would make sense if they could just think them through. "Sit and contemplate your navel," the comic farmer liked to put it. "Sit and contemplate your navel."

They sat and contemplated the government-suppressed price of wheat, which was at least a dollar per bushel lower than what it cost to produce a bushel of wheat; and contemplated *not* producing wheat as a protest; and contemplated why on earth they actually continued *to* produce wheat, losing, as they were, at least a dollar per bushel; and contemplated, finally, precisely how they were *able* still to produce wheat if they had in fact lost at least a dollar per bushel on the last hundred million or so bushels. It was this—still producing wheat—that made contemplation of the navel a somehow more reasonable and easy thing to consider. But contemplating the navel was something no one really knew anything about, and moreover, they suspected that that contemplation required a specific if not downright exotic place, and all of their place was plain.

"That goldarn government of ours," the farmer prone to comedy announced one morning to the other farmers not eating at the diner, "is *wigged out.*" Strangely coordinated, the farmers all together gently passed their clean napkins and their dimes to the waitress and wordlessly eased out of the diner. The comic farmer sat there, surprised at his foolishness in testing the expression so . . . so *blithely* a second time. He noticed that all the departing farmers wore the same co-op hat—color and apparent age of the caps looked identical. It was as if new hats had been handed out at an assembly that he had missed. This was impossible. There *were* no assemblies, certainly no hat-handing-out assemblies, and he would not have missed it if there had been such an assembly, or any kind of assembly at all. He thought immediately of alien movies: Had all his peers been possessed by . . . ? Or were they normal, and his old-hattedness an index that *he* had somehow gotten out of step? They had had a co-op party, say a wheat tour, had handed out a hundred brand-new mesh caps, and he had been somewhere else, watching TV for new material or contemplating his navel without knowing it. Kansas was becoming a strange and dangerous terrain.

He sat in the diner alone with fifty clean napkins and fifty shiny dimes.

Texas

I   I fell off the lightning rod.
I entered the sweepstakes.
I lost control.
I became beautiful.
I charmed a queen.
I defied gravity.
I moved mountains.
I bowled.
I wept, mourned, moped, and sped about town in a convertible, progressively irascing the gendarme until I was charged with exhibitionist speed.
I billed my ex-wife for lost consortium.
I filled a prophylactic with water until it was the size of the bathtub.
I let a trapped bird out of the house. Wren, I think.
I felt ill.
I felt better.
I say.

I'm alive to everything, consequently alert to nothing.

Bully, my mother would say.

I wish I dressed in light white linens through which my pink skin could be seen by the natives.

The county constabulary has a gym, and all constables weigh 300 to 400 pounds each.

I wish I were a redheaded Fort Worth millionaire ten times. I'd have a good truck, jewelry, ironed jeans, neat house, docile wife, decent daughters, bushy eyebrows, pithy maxims, damn nigh aphorisms now, and very little trouble except possibly nagging prostate. And good boots. Preferably Luccheses, settle for Sanders.

The main thing is: Don't take any shit.

That's the main thing.

The unmain thing is: You are not going to figure anything out except how to get other people to take shit, so forget about everything except not taking any yourself.

When your hair turns white, unless you are under forty, a senator, or in the movies, better punt.

If wooden rowboats would only make a comeback . . .

Girl Scout cookies, Girl Scout cookies, Girl Scout cookies.

If a boy is afraid of the dark and wets the bed, try hard, very hard, not to comment in any language.

He will grow to put you softly in your grave.

Proposition

I **Y**ou can't ramble around the woods
in your truck going to fish camps without drinking. You'll
meet up with an appointed manager of a landing that
has one or two boats go out a day, or a week, and he'll
sit you down in a chair on the lawn and sit beside you
and slap his knee and finally offer you a beer and you
will have to take it or you won't should have sat down
in the first place with such a man in such a position in
the fading, old world.

After about thirty minutes, a codger like this in such
a position—you all sitting there reading the hydrilla-
warning sign which, as much as anything else, is why
he's likely to make about only $30 from launch fees the
entire month, reading that sign for thirty minutes—he
might slap his knee again and say, "Boy, I could use
some *sex.*"

"Me too," you say, before you think very much, but
you are in it now. Brace yourself a bit, maybe try to get

another beer quick, but don't run, because a man in his position is generally highly politic.

"Do you want me to suck your dick?" he says, not reading the hydrilla sign now but looking you dead in the eye like the world's greatest salesman or priest or politician or doctor giving you the straight poop.

"Oh, naw. Thanks, but no. Thanks," you say, and read the hydrilla sign carefully.

"No shame to it, bud," he may say. "Nothing *in the world* I like better."

Basically you are looking at a grisly, lumpy man who might have changed people's oil for a living, unless he somehow got this job, which is watching the place for a rich person somewhere and taking the $1.00 from every party what runs his boat up or down the busted-up concrete slab that nobody with a heavy boat better go too far down or he'll never get out.

"Naw." You say this again and give *him* one of the earnest level-eyes and he'll get your meaning and his hopes will ebb out and you'll both be back to sign reading and stretching around in the lawn chairs and maybe you'll be ready a little earlier than you might have otherwise to get back in your truck and ramble into the woods and drink your own beer and ramble.

It might be a good thing to stop somewhere particularly scenic—maybe some young longleaf pines in clear air taking a little breeze in their rich brilliant silky sappy needles—and announce, "Perversion is pandemic." That may be a most pleasant thing to stop your rambling in the woods drinking and do.

South Carolina

[**O**n a low-country plantation, where I am invited but do not belong, there is a group of young women dressed up and going to a ball, or cotillion—if that is the word, and I doubt that it is—or even wedding, at another plantation, as happens here: you frequently go to one party in order to prepare for another party. They are in white finery that looks to me bridal but probably is just formal. One of the women is striking. She is rather small, compact, tanned, her hair back tight—she looks like an accomplished horsewoman in an evening gown; a bit out of her water but not unhappy about it. She and the other women are heading out, somewhat cattle-like, stragglers and strays but in the main accomplishing the harried exodus. I catch her eye. There is no time or place for introductions. I go up and suddenly take her by both hands firmly: "I'm quite unlikely ever to see you again."

"I've *got* to go," she says, pulling away, it seems

with only one hand, her right, which has three rings, I notice, on one finger.

"Well, put a glass slipper in the red pickup out there," I say. She leaves.

I go to the bar. It is in a large card room with a commercial big-screen television in a corner. The low-country boys do things *right*.

Someone says, "Hey, man, she's married."

I shrug. I am confident I acquitted myself brilliantly. The motif is backwards—my pickup truck among the Mercedeses is the pumpkin coach, and I should have on the slippers—but, I think, that is even better. She'll get the picture. The backwardness is a profit in irony.

At the bar I am served a beer and a parrot. You may have a parrot for your shoulder as you drink. The parrots, when served, lie on their sides on the bar, perhaps talking to you, until you pick them up. They are stored on a shelf under the bar like silverware and either can't immediately move or are trained not to.

Florida

[**H**ave: wife, child, house, dog, truck, car, boat, lake lot, annuities, IRA, shotgun, handgun, stun gun, spear gun.

Don't have: girlfriend, country home, Yazoo, liquor sideboard, anyone on retainer, condo on beach, friends.

I do not know any famous turkey guides.

I have no hope of recovering the kind of time and place that Florida was when a large rattlesnake slipped under the maid's quarters—a six-by-eight room detached from the house on Kingsley Lake, its roof, I believe, already gone, which deterred no one from calling it the maid's quarters, and inspired no one to remove or protect the maid's meager furnishings—slipped under the maid's quarters, amid the grown male hollering that accompanies the movement of all sighted snakes, got under there and holed up good, which was not too hard, because the hollering grown men did not go after him with much more than a rake handle and maybe later, inspired, a water hose on full blast, idea being that rattlesnake under maid's quarters would prefer having his head chopped off to getting wet: this kind of time and place is gone.

For one thing, I am nearly as old as the grown hollering men were then, and I do not holler at rattle-snakes, even if I could find one, and I can't. They are extinct.

Maids are out of the question.

The quarters are now a low ruin of powder-post beetle-age and funny-looking marks on the ground, as if something got nuked.

It is hot enough, generally, to think that something should *get* nuked.

The hollering men are dead, some of them, and some have new child brides and drinking problems, according to their ex-wives, and I have a drinking problem, and the maid's descendants have crack problems, or no problems except no small desire to annihilate all the descendants of the hollering men.

All of us have hope of salvation, I think, except those who actually stuck a rake handle two feet under the skirt of the maid's quarters and held it there three seconds, then ran, wondering why the rattlesnake had not obligingly attached himself to the handle for ease of magical extraction and his own execution. Some of them are still wondering.

Wait

 I   Spavined, clavicular, and cow-
hocked, with an air not of malice but simply of a leaden
determination that seemed to come up from the hard,
baking ground itself on which it stood, chained, con-
fined, gravitate to the orbit of earth depressed, moonlike,
and polished by its five-foot circular diurnal traveling,
looking forward with a low-lidded not scowl or glare but
just *look*, the eyes half-lidded and half-rolled, suggesting
not insolence or calculation or even sentience but a kind
of pride—rear-axled and log-chained for a lifetime to a
hot powdery hole in which it is its fate to consider its
chances of fighting, the rare times not chained, for its
very life—a profound self-esteem that says simply, *I am
here, you see that I am here, what need to look you in
the eye*: the bulldog bit the corncob truncate.
     Truncate?
     Into foreshortened segments, not as if—
     He busted it all up?

—not as if they had once been parts of a greater piece, but as if they could yet assemble into a piece larger, so profound was their truncation—

Dog bit the corncob?

—there, vanquished at the splayed feet of the animal with an air not canine but not unlike a locomotive, small, furred, steeled, yet without so much a train of cars behind it as the quintessence of linked and smelt earthcore, its log chain—

Dog bit the goddamned corncob?

—yes. Yes. Wait—

In *half* or *what?*

Wait. Not halved so much as *no longer whole,* as if in the authority of the bite was contained the undoing of natural history, and if there were two pieces of corncob where there had been one, there might have been now twenty; for the moral, imperative, and inviolate impression made was of a corncob no longer *one.*

In half, in the dirt?

In the moted, desiccate, rivulet ground.

I dig where you comin from, but you talkin in circles.

Helically, gyring, for the truth is never at one location but variant, even unto itself: dislocate, inchoate, rubricate of subtler chance—

God, man. *Say* it. We this far, all happen is dog done bit a corncob. I'd have me a dog done kill a horse by now, drag a man out a burning house. And you want you a mean bulldog? He gone bite a *corncob?* Shih. I seen dog so mean he bust up his water dish—a Buick hubcap! And not just once, every time you give him water. Don't even drink the water first! Whyont you let your dog bust up a bicycle with a kid on it, or bust up lawnmower, a *runnin* lawnmower—

The corncob is integral to this kind of story. You can do a lot with a corncob.

Yours is bust up.

True. You can do a lot with what can no longer happen. Thwarted fate is integral to this kind of story.

Well, integral some action in your story. Git on wid it.

Wait. Wait. Wait.

What else I can do?

Wait.

Wayne's Fate

I **G**oing up the ladder after lunch I see Wayne badly handling the stepladder we need to get to the dormer peaks and wonder how he gets away with stuff like that without falling: and then that he does not get away with it and he is falling, falls off the roof, and I wince but do not look down. I wait for the sounds. I wait clenching the ladder where I stand five rungs from the top. There is no sound. Can Wayne have found a soft canopy of tree? Has he tricked me?

I go backwards down the ladder. Not far from it, facedown, Wayne. I kneel and of course think of Rule #1: Don't move him. Then I see Rule #1 may not apply: Wayne's head is gone. This, too, looks like a trick. There is no blood or gore and from my angle, behind and to the side of him, no wound visible, just *no head*, as if he's an incomplete scarecrow.

The woman whose roof we're fixing comes out.

"Wayne fell off the roof," I tell her before she fully

reaches us, as if to prepare her for a horror that I don't want to surprise her.

"Wayne's dead," she says, and goes back in the house. She didn't know Wayne and to my knowledge had never heard his name. She has given me a lesson in hard-boil.

Of course, I say to myself. Wayne's dead, let's hard-boil. I was afraid to glance ten degrees from Wayne to look for his head. His head would have been too much. But now, hell, *Wayne's dead* and the lady is back in the house. I see her stop her daughter from running out of the house with a Popsicle. The kid has picked up a signal on its radar and is using a Popsicle to try to get through the lines. "No, you don't," her *Wayne's-dead* mom tells her, turning her with the child's momentum and aiming her back into the house.

I look around. Suddenly I *want* Wayne's head. I am its rightful finder. My previous inclination would have been to get up from where I knelt and, not looking one inch either side of Wayne, go into the house, tell the woman to call somebody, and begin drinking beer unasked from her refrigerator, and sit at her cute kitchen bar on one of her expensive blond-wood barstools and wait and drink more beer. But she has cut me off from all that. She has ruled out the feeble.

I get up and begin to look around. I stand still and survey the open ground. Wayne's head is not in the open, apparently. I change position to see behind things I can't see behind, and keep looking at the actually open ground, because that is where I'm convinced Wayne will turn up. I do not want to step on Wayne's head. This makes me take very small, shuffling steps.

Shuffling so, damned near scooting, I circle in and

out and around the compressor and the felt and the cooler and the cans of mastic. I am afraid for a moment his head will be on the sofa, and that that will be too much, will undo this steely resolve in which I scoot in figure eights about the job site looking for my partner's head. The sofa is a comic thing we do. We got it somewhere, some job, and carry it from job to job and sit on it to amuse (and enrage) customers. It's quite comfortable, except that deep down it is wet, and this will wet your clothes, so we sit on plastic. Because it got wet the sofa is ungodly heavy, too, and we have threatened to abandon it when we find a good place. I am thinking that if Wayne's head is on it, it's going to be a good place. I cannot see the seat side of the sofa and must go up and look over the back. Carefully I do this. A weird idea strikes: Wayne hit the sofa and somehow his body bounced over to where he lies now. What could have held his head?

Before looking over the back of the sofa, I see the woman at the screen door watching me. She's smoking a cigarette and has one hip out as if she's impatient with me. Her attitude somehow suggests that if I don't get on with it she's going to come out here and do it herself, find Wayne's head. She smokes like Lauren Bacall.

I look and Wayne's not on the sofa. I am as relieved as if I have found him alive. I cut a glance at the woman that has a kind of *See there?* taunt to it. She can't bully me around in my search. She can *come* out here herself if she's so smart, my next long glance at her says. I've half a mind to walk in past her and get that beer and say, "Can't find his head. Have you got a dog? Please go get some good beer, none of this Coors shit, and stop interfering with the search effort." I am getting irrationally pissed off at this woman and her problem, which was a pissant wind-only leak in her half-million-dollar Texas-fake-ranch shit house, which had to be fixed, which cost me Wayne and Wayne his head. And *Wayne's dead*, and *she* said it.

"Goddamn, lady," I say to her, but not loud enough for her to hear it. Because—things are clear now that ordinarily are not, painful things are clear—*I am afraid of her*. I suddenly see that I am afraid of everybody in the world who has any balls. This woman could be *indicted* for her undeserved wealth and asshole lassitude and I'm an honest roofer and I am afraid of her.

Wayne's head—I suddenly know where it is. I have known all along. It is in an open bucket of mastic, concealed in the stack of closed buckets, it will be there and I hope not facedown, and I know I'll never know how the body got clear over there. Maybe Wayne ran over there. Hell, he probably walked over there intending to climb back up and find the bitch's leak. He could have walked *all* around, for all I know; I was quivering on the ladder with white knuckles and closed eyes.

Wayne's head is in profile in its bed of high-quality, low-asbestos asphalt pookie. As he would be, he is grinning. He looks alive. He looks like he is whispering. I look at the woman, still smoking. Is it the same cigarette or is she smoking a carton of cigarettes watching me?

I can't hear Wayne. I kneel down.

"What?"

He says something again I still can't hear. I push the back of his head slightly into the pookie to turn his mouth up toward me.

"Tell that broad to come out here and give me a knobber," Wayne says. I start laughing.

"I will," I say. "Relax."

Never in my life have I been so *complete*. I feel like Achilles, or whoever. *The shit stops here*, I vow. I have a bunch of pookie on my hand from handling Wayne and I Go-jo it off. I put some fresh Varsol on the hand tools—there are none on the roof I know of—close the compressor, take down the ladder, put it on the truck, look in the cooler, wash the Go-jo off in the ice water, dry my hands with a clean rag, put the rag through a belt loop, and walk into the house. My hands are chilled still from the ice water and I warm them by rubbing them together. It is as though I've come in from the cold. My hands feel strong and good.

The woman has backed away as if surprised or scared.

"Have you called anyone?" I ask.

"*Called* anyone?"

"I think it's time. Let me have a beer."

She just stands there. What is this? Lauren Bacall suffers sudden loss of composure.

The refrigerator is packed with every kind of packaged food there is. Wine in the door, exotic mustards, a lot of them. Hebrew National weenies, and nobody's Jewish. The beer, when I find it, I know will be in whole, unbroken six-packs, or it will be in deli twos. I have a very good feeling about this particular fridge, though. These people are not far from Nolan Ryan, and I'll bet they know him, and if Nolan drops in, Nolan will want more than two beers, two Löwenbräus. I dig through a bushel of produce, noting the absence of iceberg lettuce. If it weren't for McDonald's, iceberg lettuce wouldn't have no luck at all. I sit down to take a longer look. Look at things from the underside. Pickle jars have a ring of little glass nibs around their lower rim, maybe for gripping? Silver-canned light Coors beer in tallboy, yes two six-packs. The woman is on the phone.

On the barstool I regard her. Not so bad.

"Who's your husband with?" I ask.

"With?" she says, smiling, I think, rather too broadly.

"Work with."

"The police are coming."

"May I ask you what the roof leak damaged?"

"It wet the floor. Awful *bleachy* kind of stains."

"I see."

Something of Achilles has been lost, but not much.

"My friend Wayne wants you to give him a knobber."

"What?"

"Nothing."

Some friend I am. Some friend I am. Some friend I am.

She *bursts* into tears. Violent sobbing that scares me. I get off the stool as if to run.

"What did you have to say *that* for?" she asks.

"Say what?"

"*I see.* In that way."

"I take it back. I *don't* see."

"My husband—" she starts, and then is overcome with hard crying. She really is not bad at all. I have a vision of eating a meal with her, steaks handsomely charbroiled on the Jenn-Air, and later holding hands strolling the cattleless ranch with her. I have a vision of almost everything. My mind is spongy. "What the hell's wrong with you?" I think to say to her, but it seems silly.

"There aren't warts on character," I tell her. "Character is nothing *but* warts. Character, ma'am, is plate tectonics. The mind is all buckle and shear, buckle and shear." She pays no attention.

"Ma'am, I hope they get here soon. And I know you do, too. Your husband might be the sort people would kidnap for money, it occurred to me, but this is not probably the sort of thing rational people can afford to worry about."

Wayne would not hurt a fly, but we had another worker once who had shot and killed a boy after a bar fight. At once I want to see him in this situation, and I do not. He would know what to do.

"Would you mind waiting outside?" I ask the woman.

"What?"

"You go outside awhile. This is *my* house."

She *does*! Just goes out.

The kid reappears, same kid with as near as I can tell same Popsicle, trotting in the same line. "No, you don't," I tell her, but she goes on in stride right out the door.

I wish Nolan Ryan *would* drop in.

The police arrive, arrest me for trespass, you figure that one. They've moved Wayne—I don't see him as I go out, but since I'd taken down the ladder it's possible I didn't look exactly in the right place, had lost the bearing.

Fear and Infinitude

I   **Y**ou are not allowed to be afraid. There is nothing to be afraid of. There is nothing, at any rate, to be afraid of that being afraid of it won't compound. We have nothing to fear but compound fear.

I'm afraid of Mrs. Jenkins. I have no idea who she is. I am certain I would be afraid of her if I knew her. The name is arbitrary.

I am afraid of success, in its full-blown forms and in its tinctures. Of failure, I used not to be afraid, but that was a pose; one embraces failure to deny success. But now I am afraid of failure, too. It is zero, or negative, success, and just as scary.

Of lunatics I am glibly, blithely unafraid. Unless they get near me, particularly if they are undiagnosed. Of lunacy I am afraid: my own. Of course. Being afraid of only the common scary things in life is scary. There is more to be afraid of, and to be *more* afraid of, than the putative fearful.

I am afraid of stupidity—as in lunacy, my own. The stupidity of others is, usually, a comfort. Not always.

It's comforting to be well off in terms of money, but even a sackful of money is a temporary phase of a sack of nothing, and therefore money can give you real creeps.

Sex. Who is not afraid of sex? One is afraid of sex outright (rare), afraid of *one kind* of sex, afraid of certain acts of sex, afraid of *not* having some kind of sex or enough sex or of not having any sex at all—of sex, who is not, somewhere, sometime, afraid?

There's a high-singing dude behind a door where I sit and have coffee right now. I doubt that he is afraid of anything at all. He's not afraid, for one thing, of sounding more like a woman than a woman can. I wouldn't be either, come to think about it, but I can't begin to do it. I'll wager—just natural laws—he's afraid of *something*, but I suspect it's trivial if it exists at all.

The trivial for me is, of course, one of the truly frightening things in the world. Again: *one's own* is the corker here, and yet one practices triviality all one's life in preparation for coming to terms with it; one trains for an entire fifteen rounds of being pronounced trivial, and then, right at the end, one relaxes and gets knocked out by the fact of one's triviality. Very scary, this bugger.

Now is a scary item if ever there was one. I have, I suspect, never not miffed the now. Now is too fast for me. Now leads to drinking. Drinking undoes now handsomely. Dismantles the whole onslaught. And in that refuge, respite of straight time, you can be afraid to come back, very very afraid. Very. Very.

I think of Mrs. Jenkins. I wish I knew her. I'd have her sexless, therefore free of that kind of fear. Yes: the only sexual fear pertaining to Mrs. Jenkins is the feeblest one: of not having any at all. *No sex with Mrs. Jenkins.* Let's establish that. It's out of the way. Of no concern, to us or to Mrs. Jenkins. Mrs. Jenkins, whatever else might plague her, is not afraid of having no sex with us either. Or with anyone. Mrs. Jenkins is, as the phrase goes, whatever it means actually (but we've established our own meaning), sexless, save for her marital relations. God, I like her already. To Mrs. Jenkins you will not sing, If you want to be a friend of mine, bring it with you when you come. You won't sing it because, if she understands it, it's bad form, and if she doesn't, it's pointless, leads to explication, embarrassing self-explication.

Embarrassment, taken to soaring heights, can be scary.

So: with Mrs. Jenkins we will observe correct manners. We are getting to know her. We are going to neither broach nor have sex with her, and we will be correct in all dealings with her. As correct as an etiquette book, if possible. Though here we will have to guess, not ever having read one, except for amusement, and then only parts, of course. One might consider reading etiquette books entire, even current ones, if they exist, and remaking oneself in their image, but I find this scary and probably unnecessary for our relationship with Mrs. Jenkins. With Mrs. Jenkins, I should think a program of simple but vigilant common decency would be sufficient. Mrs. Jenkins should not be judged boring by this prescription for our deportment with her. *We* will be boring.

Mrs. Jenkins will be so interesting she will scare you.

———

Will we want to know about her husband? Even though we ourselves are not to be sexually interested in Mrs. Jenkins, still we might, within the boundaries of common decency, determine that Mr. Jenkins is himself a cad unworthy of Mrs. Jenkins. Mr. Jenkins is probably just a middling kind of oaf very much like ourself, but he is enjoying the advantages of and therefore our vague scorn for his no-cut contract on the Mrs. Jenkins team.

Mrs. Jenkins makes love to Mr. Jenkins with a lot of jewelry on.

Mrs. Jenkins will atomize perfume into the sheets, a cloying sweetness that suggests *Ding dong! Avon calling!* and prevents you from breathing properly and makes you feel superior to people (like Mr. Jenkins) afraid of human odors and all the funky delights found beyond the gates of excess as you in your superior way regularly find and love them.

Mrs. Jenkins may even work herself out of a girdle. She may have a cellulite problem. It is possible, though, given her manner—a kind of quiet, *Come home, boy* attitude she manages by patting the mattress twice beside her hip—that Mrs. Jenkins is the most powerfully attractive woman we have ever seen and we may champ at the bit of our contract with her, that clause about not having sex with her which we agreed to early in the imagining of her, and which was necessary *for* the imagining of her, but which we now, as we smell her room odiously sweet and see her bashfully and yet boldly pat the bed beside her inviting, dimpled thighs, regret. And in that regret, within the boundaries of common decency, we assault the privileged Mr. Jenkins, who usurps our place in all that perfume.

Mr. Jenkins probably has more and better diplomas than we have, and yet has arguably not done much with them. We have done more with our few, poor certificates. Mr. Jenkins has never really not had money, and that he has not had a lot has never bothered him. Mr. Jenkins is some kind of asshole on cruise control. It would not be inappropriate, within the boundaries of common decency, if we were to lift him from his Masters-and-Johnson-guided toils upon Mrs. Jenkins by a wire garrote around his neck.

Here we would have a problem. Mr. Jenkins is the kind of guy who would, somehow, get both hands under the garrote before you hoisted him up to the ceiling and, though capable of talking, say nothing. Out of some kind of prudence, too, rather than fear. Mr. Jenkins has a manual in his head for all occasions. *The best thing to do, in case of wire garroting when making love to your wife, is, after you have inserted your hands under the garrote to prevent serious injury to your neck, say nothing to your assaulter, who anyway may be, and in many cases is, invisible. Do not try to reason with the invisible lovemaking garroter. He can be made more dangerous.*

"We will let you down if you'll talk," you tell him, but he will still just hang there, breathing a mite harder perhaps than he was moments before, his eyes very slightly widened, perhaps.

Mrs. Jenkins, *yes*: all that perfume, dimpled flesh, bangles bangling! Mr. Jenkins levitated, prudent, above us. *If the invisible lovemaking garroter assumes your position with your wife, remain calm. An outburst on your part, even a show of agitation, can be disastrous. The garroter need not, should not, for example, see you wiggle your legs or run in space above him. Hang motionless. He will forget you.*

If you could figure out what to do with the Mr. Jenkinses of the world, both before and after you've garroted them to the ceiling, you'd be a lot better off, infinitely better off, infinitely.

Labove and Son

I Labove was scared. Hard not to be, in those circumstances. I'm scared, too. My circumstances are different.

I've changed my name, to Bobby Love II. You change your name when your schemes don't work out and you move to Texas—the kook who wrote the book says so—and my father had done all but the name changing, so I added that.

One thing that will scare you is reading about your old man in a book, and scare you more if the book is not supposed to be true but is. Everything else in the book is made up, probably, but my father's part. He put a proposition to a student and she was young and he lit out, had to—there was a fat, deranged, older-brother type he was scared of, and what the book doesn't say is where he landed.

He landed in El Campo, Texas, schoolteaching, this time pawed the oldest, skinniest, safest girl in town, and had me, and I got rid of the Labove as fast as possible. My father was haunted by the memory of touching the Varner girl for all of five seconds the rest of his life. There was nothing subtle or serious about it, except that he was scared. After a time he was scared of *fruit*.

"What she was like, I need Italian to tell you," he said once. Once, he cut up a melon into pieces so small we couldn't pick them up on a knife as you might peas.

Our mother—mine; he called her Mother, too—was a stick. If the one he ran from was a melon, our mother was a vine, and she had a great calming effect on him. He'd kick back in a straight chair, front legs about one inch off the floor, regard her in a squint, standing there before us in a limp, unironed dress, and say, "Hadley, am I ever glad to see you." He might say this one hour after seeing her last. She'd stand there, with a mixing bowl on her slim hip maybe, shake her head at him, and go on with her business, which was only running the house. Thus, Labove was secure.

I saw at some early age that I was not going to be wildly successful in life. Either that, or I decided somehow at some early age not to *be* wildly successful in life. Or both, conceivably, though neither vision nor plan will I claim to have consciously held. Let me sing, a bit out of key, rudely, oh, you boring devils, for I am scared and I am Bobby Love II.

One day a fellow student in our miserable school here handed me *The Hamlet* and said, "Your father's in this book." I looked and there was a Labove pawing a child in a classroom. Funny, I thought, and I thought to borrow the book and present it, much as the kid had to me, to my father. I gave no credence to the remote possibility that the book's Labove was my father until my father looked at the book and I saw him react. The legs of the straight chair came down their one inch into a crisp, four-legged address, and the book was planted square on the table, and my father's face held six inches above it in a trance. Backwards he read, then back to his name, then forwards and backwards and forwards and forwards more, then he skipped back way before and read forwards. Half an hour later: "Is this book suitable for students your age?"

"How would I know?" I said.

"You know this is a work of *fiction*, do you not?"

"I suppose it is. Is it?" By this I meant I hadn't had time to tell if the book was a novel or what. I'd had enough time to tell it wasn't Shakespeare's *Hamlet*, and that my father's name was in it, and that the named Labove was a schoolteacher like my father.

My father was out the door. When he returned, the book was not with him. I said nothing, though I was going to have to give it back to the boy who'd borrowed it from the library. It was one of those times we are all familiar with: more was happening before me than I could guess with the aid of a hundred questions answered, so the prudent course was to ask *none*. Preserve your innocence *as is*, cut your losses, maintain the dignity of the ignorant. For two weeks the boy railed for his book. Then he came up and said, "Forget it."

Now a question: "Why?"

"Don't know. There's no fine. No record I checked it out. *No book*."

There are many libraries in the world, even the world of El Campo, Texas, in these times, and I thereupon located the nearest *Hamlet* to fall outside the zone of Labove's control. There it all is, my father and the melon-breasted child and all—if you are contemplating at any level the wildly unsuccessful life yourself—you need to know.

Four years later, when I was eighteen, I said as a joke to him, "Do you think I might change my name, legally?"

He pushed his fingers together, tip to tip, in a slow accordion motion, or if you want to see it, you can imagine one hand being a spider, albeit a five-legged spider, and the other hand being its reflection in a mirror. Now you have to wonder what a spider is doing calisthenics on a mirror for. Perhaps the spider is not doing calisthenics but is slipping. But how slowly, near meditatively, the spider is slipping, up and down, on the mirror, which mirror is held, sideways, by my father, whose hands the spider is, whose . . . one of the things you get wildly unsuccessful in, if you try, or do not try *not* to, is in your brain. Your brain can get out of hand. It can let you, or make you, paw a child, for example.

When he got through finger meditating, when the spider had pursed its mind, my father said, "Why would you want to change your name?"

"Oh," I said, "to something snappier. Less chic. Something more American, *with* it."

"I see," he said.

"*Love*," I said.

He thought for a minute and pushed back in the chair, front legs a rare full three inches off the ground. "What she was like, I need Italian to tell you. Change your name."

This I did.

Things I am scared of: words like *empyrean* and *sentience*. Ignorance in general, but not much and not often. But sometimes, bad. All people, especially children, who have the most courage. Financial newspapers, not a word of which I get. It is possible not to be afraid of your bank balance, but once it gets very low, all you can do is be afraid of it. Same with one too high. Police, of course; all law, in fact. Law is a giant web we've paid someone to erect so we can watch other people, and eventually ourselves, foul in it. Circuses I am not afraid of.

Housepainting is not scary, but the likelihood of *poor surface preparation* is very high and therefore frightening, and housepainting is therefore also. All things which someone other than yourself must be entrusted to do are frightening, and all things which you alone must do are terrifying. Getting up early in the morning.

Fishing, though, is not frightening. However: if it's any good, it's expensive, and if it's not, it's dumb.

Eleemosynary. Litigation. Lack of litigation.

Brilliant discovery.

New women, old women. Medium-known women are not frightening. But they come from the new and grade ever so hard to tell scarily into the old.

No women.

Most theory.

Death by "natural causes."

Once in a while, to be legally named Bobby Love II.

Not afraid to have my heart broken, but very afraid of thinking it broken.

Not afraid to break a heart, but very afraid to think I've broken one and haven't.

The funerals of my mother and father, Mr. and Mrs. Labove.

Lubrication schedules not adhered to.

Insurance policies. Insurance itself. We had it better when there was plague, rapine, and Gaul, and that was all you could do about it. No recourse to paper. There was blood or not blood. I would not have been sore afraid then.

Candiru worms, it goes without saying.

Courage itself is a bit frightening, of course, for you've posited its opposite, and that is fear; therefore, you've posited its opposite, lack of fear, and lack of fear is fear itself, especially when detected in others, perhaps the most fearful moment of all.

Aphorisms.

Voting.

Duty in all guises, suggestions, hints, and evil, quiet hortations.

All things beyond one's control, of course, are frightening, but the very few *within* call for duty.

And shooting from the hip. My name is Bobby Love; I sometimes call myself, and insist others do, too, *Robert*, and am curiously not afraid of pretentiousness and other forms of self-importance, for the folly is so high there is finally no joke beneath it, no failure of mind in the arrogant who lack the mentality for arrogance. My name is Bob Love II; my father pawed a thirteen-year-old bovinity of such melon-colored and abundant flesh that straps were not corralling it to the satisfaction of disguised satyrs like my poor old man. How many boys can say of their fathers, I like him? Well, I'm very afraid, more afraid than of a brain escape, a jailbreak of your wits, I am very afraid of saying I like him, *I like my old man*, who ran from a book, from a book a kook wrote who did not know him—no, he ran from a girl and the kooks that would kick him in the balls for having some, and you tell me not to be frightened? You know what is going on on this earth? Does anyone? Do you think you would not be afraid of things—can think of nothing I'm not— if your father was Labove?

Don't give me that. Not Robert Love II.

Mr. & Mrs. Elliot and Cleveland

[**M**r. Elliot had been under the natural strain that a young sculptor with a new wife and
young child and more teaching credits than sculptures
can be under. He carefully adjusted his domestic behavior to the bad so that it would substitute for the wild-
side, marginal-member-of-society behavior expected of
someone of his artistic temperament.

The large zones of non-participation—he liked to
say non-proliferation—in his domestic behavior were
anything to do with the baby, other than playing with
her, and anything to do with the house, other than sleeping in it and tending its miniature wet bar, and anything
to do with his wife's parents. The house itself had come
to mock him. It was not a castle and he was certainly
not its king.

It was a cinder-block suburban affair, beige and
white, with a nice fenced yard, three bedrooms, and
sliding glass doors to the rear patio; it was the sort of

house that people laugh at until they find themselves, somehow, in one.

Somehow for Mr. Elliot was this: his wife's parents insisted they move to a safe neighborhood. That had been that, and the beginning of Mr. Elliot's guerrilla resistance to them, the house, the wife, and the child. They, the enemy, had also, he managed to divine, decided to withhold any further aid except the rent on this safehouse, because in their opinion their daughter was too young to marry and have a child. He was forced to intuit this, and to intuit that they, the enemy, were quite well off. The pregnancy was of the accidental and overnight variety and had been more or less the *raison d'être* for the marriage, and had been certainly a *fait accompli* when all parents were notified. Consequently, he had met his wife's parents once, at the hospital, and they had visited around each other, as had his parents her parents, and his parents *him* as well, for the three days, and that was that.

Now Mr. and Mrs. Elliot were on their own except for the safehouse, which constantly assaulted him, involved him, in particulars of class warfare. A *half day* he would have to spend getting belts for a vacuum cleaner, because the house was wall-to-wall in odious carpet that was sculpted in patterns and little mountain ranges of nap or pile or whatever it was. The floor reminded him of a groomed poodle. Before the class struggle got him, he would have had *dirty floors*. It was safe for an artist to have a drink in the morning on a gritty floor, but not on a static-giving carpet which held invisible filth.

He got up one morning and found his wife eating white beans in ham stock, one of her favorite dishes and, before the house, one of his. There was a bean on the baby's chin and a bean on his wife's chin, too. She was holding the baby and could not get either bean. It set him off. The beans would have been all right over the dirty floors of a proper apartment, certainly all right in one in which he alone as an artist was eating poorly in the service of vision, but here, with . . . it all, *it set him off.* One of his big ideas rang in his head like a bell, a big bell with a big clapper: All women are whores.

He walked out of the house, wearing only his pants. He started his car and drove to the convenience store. It was not at all unusual to see shirtless, shoeless men in convenience stores in north Florida. Usually they were handsome young men working as surveyors or house framers with tanned washboard stomachs and bleached white hairs on them—Mr. Elliot called these men, or boys, cracker surfers. He did not look like them, but he did not believe he would be discriminated against because of his looks. His stomach did not suggest so much a washboard as laundry itself, and his hair, instead of the long, sun-bleached Ted-Nugent-dos, as the Florida boys themselves referred to such styles, was so thin that uncombed it gave Mr. Elliot the look of a man with a head wound.

His wife was beautiful, eating white beans at 8:30 in the morning or not. He believed she had the nastiest sexual past of any woman he'd ever known, and nastier than any he could imagine. They made great gustatory love—the word was his—but when he got up and saw her doing something like eating homemade pork and beans, and feeding the baby pork and beans, a food sold canned to the poor with a federally mandated tincture of pork in it balanced by a federally mandated maximum of rodent hair . . . if you pressed Mr. Elliot: All women were whores—he was a Catholic, he had got out of the house as soon as possible, he had had to.

He would buy a shirt by running into K mart. With the shirt on, albeit something cheap with fish-smelling dye, he'd be presentable enough to calmly stroll into SHOES and buy a pair of socks and vinyl shoes. Then some beer at the first joint open on I-10, and full recovery of dignity. It was possible that his wife had slept with her brother, and it was probable that she was the most beautiful woman in Florida or any other state shy maybe of New York, where there was unnatural transplanted beauty. He had a good car, a good solid four-door Chevrolet that would never let him down on the freeway.

When they made great gustatory love, it thoroughly and pleasantly ragged him out, and of her pleasure he had decided this: if it wasn't the best she'd ever had, it was her fault. How was he to compete with . . . with whatever was out there in the dark? That was what she had come from, smiling like an angel. He asked her out the first time he saw her, and to marry him the second. She was quite possibly pregnant by then. Woodpile, he thought, when this aspect of things drifted before him.

After the baby was born and the bloom wore off the baby, which bloom wore off proportionately to his washing off the baby's cream-bespinached bottom, he left his bean-eating ineffably attractive past-besmirched wife and Raphaelic infant and rented a $100 room and got a typewriter and decided to write it all down. The whole thing. How . . . well, the entire affair, and then some. And a lot of stuff before *that*.

It went well. There was not enough paper or beer to keep him going. It got cold and he started burning the bond paper to keep warm and kept the beer outside to keep it cold. He burned paper from the bottom of the ream and typed on it from the top, and when the two dwindling supplies met he still had beer and was conscious. He would not type on an empty platen—a fair gesture where art and soul were concerned, perhaps, but it was bad for a typewriter to type on an empty platen. The money he had left was not enough for another ream of paper but was enough for another case of beer. He got that and many newspapers—financial ones were the best paper value—and burned them and drank beer and thought the rest of his novel, as he was calling it, through.

It was good, he knew. Writing the rest of it would be no problem. Two days later, it was not good. There was no point in finishing it. He began burning the extant portion, which relieved the demand on fuel money and released funds for more beer. It got even colder.

He called on a woman he knew and they went out. They went back to her place, where Mr. Elliot, expecting her to be anticipating the whole hog, took his clothes off in her kitchen and passed out. The woman called his wife, who came over in the morning. They both studied Mr. Elliot, fetally coiled on the linoleum.

"I'm sorry," Mrs. Elliot said.

"You should be," the woman said. She was black and she was confused by all this in a way she would not have been if Mr. Elliot had been on her floor and black. "I didn't mean it like that," she added. "My name's Cleveland."

Mrs. Elliot wondered what she did mean, and Cleveland wondered what she had meant, too. Mrs. Elliot did not want to find out. She knew enough to let a black woman named Cleveland with someone else's white husband passed out on her kitchen floor think whatever ill she wanted. Cleveland, for her part, though, wanted to find out what she had meant by her own rudeness.

"Let's have some coffee. He hasn't blocked the stove." Mr. Elliot whimpered and his hands quivered. "He looks like a dog dreaming." They both laughed.

Cleveland put condensed milk and more sugar— five teaspoons—in her coffee than Mrs. Elliot thought physically possible. Will it dissolve? she wondered, sipping hers black. She declined additives herself. She sat there in a state of mind that may be fairly and accurately abridged *weirded out*. She could not think of appropriate things. That was the fault, or the price, she thought, of being there at all when you should have called an ambulance or the police on your alleged husband and got out. She had imprudently ignored judgment and the madly whispering voice of sense and sat down for coffee. "I'll need no sugar, thanks," she said to Cleveland, thinking: Yours will somehow sweeten mine.

Mrs. Elliot hoped several things while Cleveland finished up her thick stirring. She hoped Mr. Elliot would not come to. She hoped she would not ask, or find out, what he was doing there. She hoped this Cleveland had better sense than to ask questions herself. She wanted to just sit there and have coffee in the sunny little dining room like a couple of housewives in their mid-morning lull.

"What is that?" Cleveland asked.

"What?"

"What you're humming."

"Was I humming?"

"I know the song but can't think of it."

"I didn't know I was humming."

"Ah," Cleveland said. "Are you in school?"

"Yes."

"Which one?"

Mrs. Elliot told her. Cleveland was a graduate student at the same school. In the same department in which Mrs. Elliot was an undergraduate and in which Mr. Elliot taught. This explained their sipping coffee together a room away from where Mr. Elliot whimpered naked on the floor.

"Well," Cleveland said. "Enough of that." Then she announced, "You *are* beautiful," and slapped her knee.

This should have been odd but was not. Mr. Elliot had talked some before retiring, it would seem. It made perfect sense. Mrs. Elliot's beauty was something she no longer was self-conscious about. She had never *used* it, but she had been for a while embarrassed by it and tried to slough it off. Now she accepted it. Cleveland accepted it. How had her soft-bellied passed-out husband had the grace to go rutting on an *intelligent* woman?

Cleveland stood up and stretched. "I think I have tendonitis, or something," she said, and sat back down.

"Did you play volleyball?" Mrs. Elliot asked.

"No. Tall enough, but didn't. It wasn't . . ."

"Yeah."

"How'd you hook up with him in there?"

"He was cute."

"You want more coffee?"

"Yes."

When Cleveland came back with the coffee she said, "Safe and sound. I'll hand you that, he's cute."

"He's cute."

They both laughed again.

"God Almighty," Cleveland said.

"Do I leave, try to take him, or what?"

"Just leave. I will, too. He'll get up on his own self."

Mrs. Elliot said, "You've been . . . correct."

Cleveland looked at her and said nothing.

Mr. Elliot after that was his own master. He was in control. He was prescribed some medicine designed to address polar-brain disorder, which one doctor said he had, and some other medicine to block beta waves, which another doctor, laughing at the first, said he had too many of. He took the one medicine, then the other, then both, then neither, and went back to beer.

When he moved back in, which he did in a straight line from the linoleum floor of Cleveland's kitchen, saying to Mrs. Elliot only "Whew. Rough night," and nothing of the week he'd been gone before that, writing his novel and burning it, both before and after it was on the page, he delivered himself of a speech.

"I will be a good husband," he said. "And observe these rudiments of good-husband behavior. I will—" He stopped and said, "Here," taking from his jacket—which he noticed at that moment he had never seen before, how remarkably well it fit, and it appeared to be well made—a note. He handed the note to Mrs. Elliot. It said, in pencil:

I WILL NOT
wash dishes
 "   *diapers*
vacuum house
sweep   "

mind baby
feed   "
clean   "   's ass
give dinner parties
go to   "   "
entertain in-laws
visit   "
tolerate   "
talk on
phone with "
receive mail at this address

Mrs. Elliot read the list and walked to him and kissed Mr. Elliot, which he did not expect.

"Be as bad as you can be, honey," she said to him. "It won't amount to much." He could feel and taste her lipstick.

Mr. Elliot's astonishment was not as large or long-lasting as he felt it should have been. His first thought: All women *are* whores! Mrs. Elliot in that little nick of time had left the room and was coming back through it with one arm full of baby and one arm full of laundry. She smiled on her way through.

The smile was a guileless, almost radiant, but finally just naturally pleasant expression on the face which was the most beautiful face he had ever seen at close range to conceal the worst past he had ever fathomed at long range. What *was* she?

Am I out of . . . bounds? Am I in the ball game?

Thoughts like these were not common to Mr. Elliot. "None of us knows what the ball game is" was a notion that he commonly embraced. Yet the idea that the game was known but somehow not *to him* was a strange and unhappy, feral thought with tusks on it.

He wouldn't clean the baby's ass or talk to her parents and she could say *it didn't amount to much?* He suddenly had one of his visions of her: She was dancing naked in a cage in a club in a Navy area in Jacksonville. *Gyrating* did not quite do her salacious whirling and spine-whipping justice. He got a grip on the kitchen counter and waited for the seizure to pass and hoped nothing blew out. He was afraid to feel the jacket for pills. He was afraid of the pills. He was afraid of about everything in these visions except the floor immediately beneath his feet, which in this case was kitchen linoleum that also scared him because of his having inexplicably waked up on some of it that morning.

He calmed himself. These visions, if you wanted to call them that, were what informed him of his wife's nasty sexual past. He did not know where they came from. That is to say, his wife had not told them to him, nor had anyone else. Which did not reduce their claim on him a bit, or their . . . *mythical* truth. They were like the Harpies, as if he were . . . whoever the old fart was they snatched the food from. Every time he saw his wife as an angel, as *way* better than something good enough to eat, these things came from the sky screeching *No you don't* and fouling the air and somehow instilling in the prospect of his beautiful wife an odor utterly rancid. And while you could not say where these Harpies came from, or ascribe any reason why they were coming as you starved to death, you also could not say they were not, in important senses, *real.*

———

In his kitchen, his wife humming in the laundry room, Mr. Elliot was still recovering from the naked-dancing vision. He tried reasoning some more. He had disappeared for a week, he gave her his list, she kissed him and started laundry. All right. There was something domestically pliable or reliable enough in her that belied her having danced naked in a cage. Or argued for it. Only someone who had weathered—or enjoyed—the pawing (and?) of the denizens of, say, the Comic Book Club, sailors off ships, would find his own trials amounting to *not much.*

Mr. Elliot groaned audibly in the kitchen. He could not cry. He was beyond that. He started tapping his foot.

He was hearing, from the laundry room, Mrs. Elliot, who was humming and singing, somewhat, a song, to the rhythm of the washing machine. Her voice was not good, but at any rate she was not so much singing as talking the lyrics, as if trying to recall them.

> *And if that mockingbird don't sing,*
> *Somebody gonna buy me a diamond ring.*

Mr. Elliot was further stricken, if that were possible. Was she *mocking him?* How had she come up with this business of a bird in a cage—the only way you could *have* a mockingbird—and why a *mocking*bird just as he had had his attack of seeing *her* in a cage? Had she *sent* the Harpies of go-go? The myth surfaced: He was King Phineus, blind at a stone table, reaching for roast lamb and stuffed vine leaves and getting flapped in the face by leering, stinking birds.

"What's that song, *dear?*" he asked.

"What song?"

"You were singing."

"I was singing?"

Ho! She did not have the courage to kill him openly and cleanly. She was doing more capework. Mr. Elliot walked into the laundry room with violence—which he had never effected and only once himself been a minor victim of—uppermost in his mind. He hummed the tune, as menacingly as he could.

Mrs. Elliot, smiling at him, picked the tune up and hummed herself. Mr. Elliot, who thought he should hit her, wanted suddenly to kiss her, badly.

"Oh that," Mrs. Elliot said. "You know what? I can't figure the sense of having a *mocking*bird in there. It seems to mock the sentimentality of the song itself, doesn't it? Is that possible? Could it be that sophisticated?"

Could she? was all Mr. Elliot could think. Enough to send the caged woman, the caged bird, the mockery . . . she looked delicious! She was taking his hand. She put it with hers into the open washing machine, down into the hot suds and clothes, and their hands swung together in the reversing half-circle motion.

Then Mrs. Elliot *held* his hand—not simply in there, but held it as if they were *holding hands*. As if, remove the washing machine, they were new to each other and at the movies.

"I knew a boy did this with his feet once and the thing went into spin," Mrs. Elliot was saying. Mr. Elliot had a dreamlike look on his face, so she waited before telling the story.

Mrs. Elliot thought of the woman Cleveland, who was real. She looked at the cute lout whose hand she was holding, who was determined to be real, who did not know that if she held his hand long enough where it was he'd lose his arm. Maybe Cleveland could explain the mockingbird business. She was pretty sure the song was Motown.

"What happened?" Mr. Elliot asked.

"It went into spin, broke everything below his waist." Mr. Elliot eased his hand out of the tub.

Mr. Elliot had a grateful and self-pitying look on his face as if he was about to blubber. But this was not his emotion. He was confused, confused and happy, happy and confused and happy. He wanted to sing the song, too, but Mrs. Elliot, who had the baby asleep in one arm and Mr. Elliot with the other, was taking them both to bed.

The Winnowing of Mrs. Schuping

[**M**rs. Schuping lived on a moribund
estate that had once been grand enough in trees alone
that a shipbuilder scouting live oaks in the eighteenth
century had bought the tract for wood to make warships
for the British Navy. Oak of that sort, when fitted and
shipped into six-inch walls, would not merely withstand
or absorb cannonballs but repel them a good way toward
their source. Mrs. Schuping did not know this, but she
knew she had big old trees, and she patted their flanks
when she strolled the grounds.

The house had died. So slatternly, so ratty was it
that Mrs. Schuping was afraid to enter it again once she
had worked up the courage to go out of it, which was
more dangerous. She had been hit by boards twice while
leaving the house but never when going in.

There was no such thing as falling-down insurance,
an actuarial nicety that flabbergasted and enraged Mrs.
Schuping. Falling down was what really plagued houses,

therefore that was what you could not protect them from by lottery.

She called herself *Mrs.* Schuping arbitrarily. She had no husband nor had she ever found in the least logical the idea of having one man whom you so designated. Wholly preposterous.

She had a good toaster. It was a four-slice commercial stainless square job, missing its push-down knobs, so that you had to depress the naked notched metal thingies to lower the bread. It looked like you'd need a rag to protect your hand, but you did not. Perhaps if you were hustling breakfasts in a good diner you might, but not slowly, at home. Life was winnowing for Mrs. Schuping.

When she bought the house, she had found a huge collection of opera records, of which she knew nothing except that they sounded ridiculous. This collection she played dutifully, over and over, until it was memorized, until it could not be said that she was ignorant of opera. When she had mastered the collection, she wondered why, and she sailed the records, one by one, into the swamp behind the rotting house. She winnowed the collection of opera records until it was a collection of cardboard boxes, and eventually used those to set her first swamp fire.

Setting the swamp on fire was not a winnowing of her life, but it did winnow the swamp. The burnings seemed to her rather naughty and frivolous, and surprisingly agreeable to look at and to smell. She took an un-adult pleasure in them, along with an adult fear that she might be somehow breaking the law even though the swamp was hers.

The second time she set the mangy tangled tract on

fire the sheriff showed up, and she became sure it was the case that you could not burn your own swamp. The sheriff, whom she had not met before, confirmed her anxiety with his opening remark.

"Your *swamp* is on fire," he said, standing about fifteen feet off her right shoulder and slightly behind her.

She turned to him and said, not knowing what in hell else she might, "Yes it is."

The sheriff stood there regarding first her and then the swamp and the fire, which gave his face a jack-o'-lantern-orange sheen, and said again, "The swamp is *on fire*." The emphasis was meant to confirm his sympathies with having fires, and upon establishing that bond he walked briskly to Mrs. Schuping's side and planted his feet and crossed his arms and cocked back to watch the fire with her in an attitude that suggested he would be content to watch for a good long while. When he breathed, his belt and holster creaked.

Mrs. Schuping could not tell if his affection for the fire was genuine or a trap of the infamous misdirectional-innocuous-talk type of country police.

So she said two things. "Sheriff, I set my opera-collection boxes on fire; I confess they were in the swamp." Then, "Sheriff, I do not need a man."

The sheriff looked at the fire, followed it up into the high parts, where it licked at the grapevines climbing on the tupelo gums. It was a hot yellow heat in the slack black-ass muddy gloom of a nothing swamp that needed it. He had been taking pure aesthetic enjoyment from the thing until Mrs. Schuping said what she said, which reminded him that they were not free to enjoy this may-hem and that he had to undo her concern with his presence. Concern with his presence was—more than his actual presence—*his job* ordinarily; it was how he made his living. This was the hardest thing about being sheriff: you could not go off duty. A city cop could. They even provided locker rooms and showers for them; and he imagined laundry and dry-cleaning takeout services for the uniforms. But a sheriff was the sheriff, and he was always, always up to something. That is why he had had to talk like a fool to this woman to get her to let him watch her fire with her. How else excuse standing in front of five burning acres and saying "on fire"? But it had not worked. And this *man* thing.

"Mizz Shoop, I just—"

"It's Schuping," Mrs. Schuping said.

"Yes'm. I know. I just like to call you Shoop, though."

With this the sheriff again squared off, with a sigh, to watch the fire, whatever he had been about to say cut off by Mrs. Schuping's correcting him. He hoped he had begun the dismantling of her concerns with his presence, both legal and sexual. He was aware that he had not done much toward either end, but he did not want to babble while watching a good fire. Unless she asked him off the property, he'd hold his ground.

Mrs. Schuping was content, having posted her nolo contendere on the fire and her no desire on the man, to let him stand there and breathe and creak if he wanted to. She had been a little hard on the sheriff, she thought. It was the legal part that worried her into overstating the sexual part. Not *overstating*, *mis*stating: she did not need a man, but wanting was another question. And if all you had to do to get a big creaking booger like this one was set your back yard on fire, she was all for it.

———

Four months later the sheriff and Mrs. Schuping had their second date. He saw the smoke from the interstate, where he was parked behind the Starvin' Marvin billboard at such a ridiculous pitch that takeoff was nearly vertical and he resisted blasting off for speeders unless provoked entirely. What had been provoking him entirely lately was college kids with their feet out the windows of BMWs, headed for Dade County, Florida, with their socks on. That was making him strike, lift-off or no lift-off. He wondered what it was like for a bass. How some lures got by and some did not. For him it was *pink socks*. In the absence of pink socks, there was smoke over the Fork Swamp.

Mrs. Schuping looked even more fire-lovely than she had at the first fire. This time she saw him before he spoke.

"There won't be a problem with the permit," the sheriff said, instead of the idiocies of last time. There was no problem with the permit because there was no permit, but he thought this was a good way to address those concerns of hers.

The sheriff had lost a little weight. Mrs. Schuping had been on intellectual winnowing excursions, and she saw as a matter of vector analogy the trajectory of the sheriff toward her and the swale of her sexual self. He had a swag or a sway—something—of gut that suggested, even if a bit cartoonishly, a lion. This big fat tub could get on *top* of her, she thought, with no identifiable emotion, looking at the crisp, shrieking, blistering fire she had set with no more ado than a Bic lighter jammed opened and a pot she didn't want anymore full of gasoline.

The sheriff took a slow survey of the fire, which was

magnificent, and loyal—her little swamp was neatly set on a fork of creeks so that the fire could not get away— and turning back he caught a glance of Mrs. Schuping's profile as she watched the fire and, he thought, him a little, and down a bit he saw her breasts, rather sticking out and firm-looking in the dusky, motley, scrabbled light. Bound up in a sweater and what looked like a salmon-colored bra, through the swamp smoke stinging your eyes, on a forty-year-old woman they could take your breath away. He made to go.

"Good cool fire, Mizz Shoop," the sheriff said. "I've got to go."

"You're leaving, Sheriff?"

"It's business, purely business."

To the sheriff she seemed relaxed, legally, and there is *nothing* like a big Ford *pawhooooorn* exit—a little air, a little air and a little time.

Mrs. Schuping had been through every conscious-ness and semiconsciousness and unconsciousness and raised- and lowered-consciousness program contributing to every good conscience and bad conscience and middle struggling conscience there is. But now she was a woman in a house so falling apart the children had taken it off the haunted register, and she was boiling an egg on a low blue flame. Outside were the large, dark, low-armed oaks.

Also outside, beyond the oaks, were the smoldering ignoble trees. The white, acrid, thin smoke drifting up their charred trunks was ugly. The swamp had powers of recovery that were astounding, though. It was this mag-ical resilience that confirmed Mrs. Schuping as an avid swamp burner. When the swamp came back hairier than it had been before the burning, thicker and nastier, she found the argument for necessary periodic burning, which was of course a principle in good forestry. She was not a pyromaniac, she was a land steward. The trees stood out there fuming and hissing and steaming. Her life continued to winnow.

Beyond the disassembly of her opera holdings, Mrs. Schuping had gradually let go of her once prodigious reading. She had read in all topical lay matters. She had taught herself calculus, and could read *Scientific American* without skipping the math. She taught herself to weld and briefly tried to sculpt in metal. She gave this up after discovering that all she wanted to sculpt, ever, was a metal sphere, and she could not do it.

She had dallied similarly in hydroponics, artificial intelligence, military science, and dress designing. She had read along Great Book lines and found them mostly a yawn, except for the Great Pornography Books, for which there seemed to be no modern equivalent. She had stopped going out to concerts and movies, etc., which she had done specifically to improve herself, because it got to where after every trip on the long drive back to the ruined estate she wondered what was so damned *given* about improving oneself. The opposite idea seemed at least as tenable. As her tires got worse, it seemed even more tenable, and she began to embrace the idea of winnowing: travel less, do less, it *is* more. She found a grocery that still delivered, and she picked up her box of groceries on the front porch—as far as the boys would go.

At first she regretted the winnowing, but then she did not: she had had a mind, but nothing had properly got in its way. That happens. The same for bodies: there were good athletes in this world who had never had the right field or the right ball get in their way. It was particle physics when you got down to it, and the numbers of people in the world today and the numbers of things to occupy them made the mechanics of successful collision difficult. So she'd burn her swamp, pat her good trees, cook her egg. She had one old clock radio, a GE in a vanilla plastic cabinet with a round dial for a tuner, which she played at night. If there were storms, she listened to the static of lightning.

When the swamp had returned in its briary vitriolic vengeance, reminding her of a beard coming out of a face that was too close to hers, she set it afire a fourth time. The fire went taller than before, so she walked around to the front of the house to see if you could see it from there, and, if you could, if it looked like the house was on fire, and there was the sheriff, parking his car.

He rolled down the window and said, "I've got you two puppies." She looked in at the front seat and saw that he did. All puppies are cute, but these seemed abnormally cute. She discarded, immediately, protest. She was not going to be the sort, no matter how holed up and eccentric, to refuse a dog because of the responsibility and other nonsense.

"What kind are they?"

"The kind dogfighters give me just before they have themselves a convention." The sheriff opened the door and let the puppies out and got out himself. They all walked back to the fire. At one point the sheriff misjudged the ground and veered sharply into Mrs. Schuping and nearly knocked her down. He was so big and tight that he felt like the oak walls of the ships that flung cannonballs back, which Mrs. Schuping did not know had made her trees, under which they now walked, attractive to a shipbuilder two hundred years before.

The fire was a good one. There was a screaming out of human register as oxygen and carbon clawed each other to pieces, going through peat and leaf and the dirt that somehow stayed up in the leaves, even when it rained, giving the swamp its dusty look that would never be right for *National Geographic*. The dirt in the trees presumably turned to glass, and maybe that was why, Mrs. Schuping thought, the fire always sounded like things breaking. Tiny things breaking, a big fiery bull in the shop.

Without an inkling of premeditation, she turned to the sheriff, who was breathing and creaking there in standard fashion, and balled her fist, and very slowly brought it to his stomach and ground it mock-menacingly into him as far as it would go, which was about an inch. At this the sheriff put his hand on the back of her neck and did not look from the fire. They regarded the fire in that attitude, and the puppies romped, and in the strange orange light they looked posed for a family portrait at a discount department store.

Before going into the house, the sheriff knocked the mud off his boots, then decided that would not do and took his boots off and left them outside the back door on the porch. Mrs. Schuping put two eggs on to boil. The sheriff, who she thought might go three hundred pounds, should not eat an egg, she knew, but it was what you ate after a swamp fire—boiled hard, halved, heavy salt and pepper, and tasting somehow of smoke—and it was all she had, anyway.

They peeled the eggs at the metal table and put the

shells in the aluminum pot the eggs had cooked in. Mrs. Schuping peeled hers neatly, no more than four pieces of shell, but the sheriff rolled his on the table under his palm until it was a fine mosaic. He rubbed the tiny bits of shell off with his thumb.

When the sheriff came out of the bathroom and stood by the bed, Mrs. Schuping became frightened beyond the normal, understandable apprehensions a woman can have before going to bed with a new man, especially the largest one it is conceivable to go to bed with. She also had a concern for the bed itself, and even for the structural capacity of the house—but that was hysterical; the sheriff was safely upstairs, and no matter what he did he would not get any heavier. Something else frightened her. It was as if a third party were in the room, a kind of silent presence, and then she realized what it was. The sheriff, naked, without his creaking leather, was quiet for the first time, a soundless man. It gave her goose bumps.

"Get in."

Mrs. Schuping decided it was best to trust a man this large in the execution of his own desire and let him near-smother her. He made a way for air for her over one of his shoulders and began what he was about, which seemed to be an altogether private program at first but then got better, until she could tell the sheriff was not simply a locomotive on his own track, and things got evenly communal, traces of smoky fire in the room, but enough air. Mrs. Schuping thought of winnowing and sailing records and her mother and of how long a gizzard has to cook to be tender, how much longer than a liver, and she lost track until she heard the sheriff breathing, about to die like a catfish on a hot sidewalk, and stop.

"Mizz Shoop," the sheriff said, when he could talk, "this is my philosophy of life and it proves it. Almost everything can happen. Yingyang."

"What would be an example, Sheriff?"

"Well—this," he said, his arms arcing in the space over them and reballasting the bed. "And did you hear about them boys killed that girl for p—— Excuse me. For sex?"

The sheriff then related the details of a rape case he had worked on. It was not the sort of talk she expected to follow a First Time, but she let him go on and found that she did not mind it. The sheriff had set in motion the pattern of rude and somewhat random speech that would follow their lovemaking in the high springy bed under the ripped ceiling. You would be allowed to say whatever was on your mind without regard to etiquette or setting. Once, it embarrassed her to recall, she declaimed apropos of nothing while they were still breathless, "Listen. I have a father and a mother. I'm a *real person.*"

To this the sheriff firmly rejoined, "I think the whole goddamn country has lost its fucking mind."

"I don't doubt it," Mrs. Schuping said.

They could talk like this for hours, their meanings rarely intersecting. The last thing the sheriff said before leaving that first night was "Fifty pounds in the morning. They'll be all right under the porch." Mrs. Schuping slept well, wondering fifty pounds of what under the house before she drifted off.

The sheriff had initiated a pattern with this remark, too, but she did not know it. She would find that the sheriff was given to talking about things that he did not bother to preface or explain, and that she preferred not asking what the hell he was talking about. Whatever the hell he was talking about would become apparent, and so far the sheriff had delivered no unwanted surprises. She saw just about what she was getting.

In the river of life's winnowing, the sheriff represented a big boulder in the bed of the dwindling stream. It eventually would be eroded from underneath and would settle and maybe sink altogether. Mrs. Schuping, therefore, did not find the facts of her aggressively winnowing life and the solid, vigorous mass of her new man to be in conflict at all.

She had never known a man so *naturally* unrefined. Despite his bulk, the sheriff gave her a good feeling. That was as specific as she could be about it. He gives me a good feeling, she thought, marveling at the suspicious simplicity of the sentiment.

She had a dream of going into the swamp and finding her opera records, unharmed, and retrieving them and playing them for the sheriff, who as his appreciation of them increased began to dance with her in a ballroom that somehow appeared in her house, the operas having become waltzes, and who began to lose weight, becoming as slender as a bullfighter; then, in the swamp again, she found the records hung in the trees and melted into long, twisted shapes that suggested, of all things, the severely herniated intestines of a chimpanzee she had once seen in a cheap roadside wild-animal attraction. She woke up glad to wake up. She would look for no records and wish no diet upon the sheriff. "Have my *head* examined," she muttered, getting out of bed.

In a very vague way Mrs. Schuping had decided— before the decisions and lack of decisions that set her life

on its course of winnowing—that having one's head examined was going to be the certain price if she did not
begin to clear a few, or many, things out of it. She saw
at the end of theories of consciousness and lay physics
and broad familiarity with things topical and popular a
wreck of the mind, her mind, on the rocks of pointless
business and information. None of that knowledge, good
or bad, simple or sophisticated, was ever going to allow
her to do anything except more of *it*: drive another eighty
miles to another touring concert or exhibition, read another article on the mating dynamics of the American
anole.

She decided that a green lizard doing pushups with
his little red sailboard coming out of his throat was one
thing, but if she *read* about it anymore, saw any more
stylized drawings of "distensible throat flaps" on vectors
heading for each other like units in a war game, she was
going to be in trouble. This was a petty, flighty kind of
fed-upness to reach, and not carefully thought out, she
knew, but she did not care. If you looked carefully at bee
No. W-128, which was vibrating at such and such a
frequency, wagging its butt at 42 degrees on the compass
. . . God. Of all her pre-winnowing interests, this arcane
science was her favorite, yet, oddly enough, it was the
first to go. It had looked insupportable in a way that, say,
Time magazine had not. Yet over the years she had decided, once *Time* etc. had also been abandoned, that the
lizards and bees and flow mechanics were supportable in
the extreme by comparison—as were the weirdly eclectic
opera records more justified than the morning classical-
music shows on public radio—but once she had opted
for winnowing there was no pulling back. "I'm going
beyond Walden," she told herself, and soon thereafter

began eyeing the cluttered swamp, which was not simple enough.

So she winnowed on pain of having her head examined. If it were to be, she wanted them to find nothing in it. She knew enough about the process. Her mother had had *her* head examined, many times. Mrs. Schuping did not like her mother, so that was all she needed to know about having her head examined. Not for her.

She looked out the window that morning and saw a man with a white stripe down each pant leg walk away from the house and get in a yellow truck, which then drove off. When she investigated she found a fifty-pound sack of dog food on the porch and the two puppies scratching at it very fast, as if they would dig in spoonfuls to China.

After their first night together, the sheriff arrived without Mrs. Schuping's having to set the swamp on fire. The sheriff had established the two things he would do for or to Mrs. Schuping. One was talk trash in bed and the other was supply her with goods and services that came through his connections as sheriff. After the dog food, which had belonged to the county police dogs until her puppies got it, a crew of prisoners showed up one morning and painted the entire porch, which surrounded her house, with yellow road paint, giving the house the look of a cornball flying saucer about to take off. The sheriff appeared that night—the fluorescent paint job more than ever inspectable then—beaming with pride. He did not remark upon it directly or ask Mrs. Schuping how she liked it, but from his face, which in its pride nearly partook of the same yellow glow, it was obvious that he was sure she liked her hideous new paint job. She could not deny it.

She had watched the crew from a lawn chair, drinking coffee while they changed her haunted-looking, unpainted, unannounced house into something like ballpark mustard with mica in it, and never had asked them what they thought they were doing. Nor had she asked the man with the shotgun what he was doing. And now it did not seem proper to ask the sheriff. The dog food was done, the porch under which the puppies were to live was done, and something else would be done, and it was in the spirit of winnowing to let it be done.

But in bed that night, before they got to the sheriff's spontaneous trash talking, she did let out one question.

"Listen," she said. "Isn't this, prisoners and—" She made a kind of scalloping motion with her hand in the air, where he could see it. "I appreciate it, but isn't it . . . *graft* or something?"

The sheriff took a deep breath as if impatient, but she already knew he would not, if he were impatient, show it; he was a man who could talk about rape in bed, but in other important ways he was a gentleman. He was breathing to compose.

"If you see something I have," he said, "there is something behind it I have given." He breathed for a while.

"Law is a series of *deals*," he said next, "and so is law enforcement." More breathing. "Nobody in law enforcement, unlike *law*, makes money *near* what the time goes into it."

They looked at the ceiling.

"If you don't do Wall Street, this is how you do it."
A deep sigh.

"That dogfighter I got your puppies from made fifteen thousand dollars the next week in one *hour*, and I let him do it, and I did not take a dime. You have two good dogs he would have knocked in the head. He is a homosexual to boot."

Mrs. Schuping was sorry she had asked, and never did again. But if she saw the sheriff studying something about the place she might attempt to steer him off. He seemed to look askance at her mixed and beat-up pots and pans one night, and, fearful that he would strip the county-prison kitchen of its commercial cookware—perhaps inspired by the odd presence of her commercial toaster—and stuff it all into hers, she informed him casually that broken-in pots were a joy to handle.

She missed his siting for the deck and the boardwalk into the swamp, however, and the one clue, mumbled in his sleep, "Ground Wolmanized, that'll be hard," she did not know how to interpret until the ground-contact-rated, pressure-treated posts were being put in the yard behind her house and on back into the swamp by black fellows with posthole diggers and the largest, shiniest, knottiest, most gruesome and handsome arms she had ever seen.

She watched them, as she had watched the house-painters, this time putting brandy in her coffee—something she had tried once before and not liked the taste of. Sitting there drinking spiked coffee, she felt herself becoming a character in the gravitational pull of the sheriff despite, she realized, efforts nearly all her life not to become a character—except for calling herself Mrs. Schuping.

The boardwalk through the thinned swamp looked miraculous, as if the burning had been a plan of architectural landscaping. The handsome, lean swamp, the walk suggesting a miniature railroad trestle going out into it, resembled a park. If you winnowed and got down pretty clean and were normal, she thought, and something happened—like a big-bubba sheriff and thousands of dollars of windfall contracting and a completely different kind of life than you had had—and you started becoming a character, and you paid nothing for it and did not scheme for it, and it reversed your winnowing, and you liked brandy suddenly, at least in coffee, while watching men who put classical sculpture to shame, was it your fault?